UNIFO...

'Stand up. I'm not going to arrest you. I'm going to spank you.'

Just to get the words out of my mouth was like an electric shock. My skin was prickling all over and I already felt hot between my legs, but – it's hard to describe – just having my uniform on made me feel as if I was in armour. He had stood up, but he was completely taken aback, his face working in surprise for quite a bit before he could get the words out.

'You're having a laugh!'

'No,' I told him, 'and, besides, I thought you said you liked a bit of swish?'

He didn't know what to say. His mouth opened and closed but no sound came out. As I closed the door behind me I knew I had him. The risk of other people hearing didn't occur to me, nothing like that. I wanted it, and I wanted it then and there. I sat down on his bed, struggling to look calm and absolutely raging inside. My legs were stuck out, making a lap, the same way I'd been used to spanking Danny when we were together, but Mac didn't move.

'Come on,' I urged. 'Get over my knee.'

UNIFORM DOLLS

Aishling Morgan

The LAST
WORD *in*
FETISH

nexus

enthusiast

This book is a work of fiction.
In real life, make sure you practise safe, sane and
consensual sex.

First published in 2007 by
Nexus Enthusiast
Nexus
Thames Wharf Studios
Rainville Rd
London W6 9HA

A catalogue record for this book is available from the
British Library.

www.nexus-books.com

Typeset by TW Typesetting, Plymouth, Devon

Printed and bound in Great Britain by CPI Bookmarque,
Croydon CR0 4TD

The paper used in this book is a natural, recyclable product made
from wood grown in sustainable forests. The manufacturing
process conforms to the regulations of the country of origin.

ISBN 978 0 352 34159 4

Distributed in the USA by Holtzbrinck Publishers, LLC,
175 Fifth Avenue, New York, NY 10010, USA

Acknowledgements

To Ishmael Skyes and the London Corporal Punishment School, to the posters of Informed Consent and other boards, to Leia, Brian, Lucy, Steve and all those others who have contributed to our knowledge and understanding of the pleasures of uniform fetishism; thank you.

Symbols key

 Corporal Punishment

 Female Domination

 Institution

 Medical

 Period Setting

 Restraint/Bondage

 Rubber/Leather

 Spanking

 Transvestism

 Underwear

 Uniforms

One

It's not often you get to see an air hostess take her knickers down in public.

She had turned her back to us, her eyes full of mischief and teasing as she took hold of her uniform skirt. I still wasn't sure she'd go through with it, despite her promises, an uncertainty which made it all the more exciting as she slowly eased her skirt up her legs. My eyes followed the seams of her stockings, slowly upwards, glad to see every inch of thigh and praying for more. And I got it – the patterned lace of her stocking tops, the gentle bulges of flesh above them, her suspender straps, a hint of white where her knickers tucked under, a little well-rounded bottom flesh, and more.

Her smile was pure impudence as she stuck her bottom out and put the seat of her knickers on show, plain white cotton pulled taut over her small pert cheeks. My heart jumped at the thought of them coming down, and what she'd be showing if she did, but I wasn't at all sure it was going to happen. She seemed content to tease, swaying her hips gently as she watched us from those big languid eyes, revelling in the power she held over us.

Even what she was showing had given the audience quite a shock. Her uniform was the real thing, not sexualised at all, and she'd started with a comic sketch, so they'd assumed she was a comedienne and nothing more. Even then she'd have been worth watching. Slender, tall and immaculately turned out, she had that blend of the pretty and the purposeful one hopes for in an air hostess, a style set off to perfection by her uniform.

It was a pale blue-grey, in fine wool cut to follow the contours of her body, so that her skirt accentuated the shape of her hips and her jacket made her waist seem slimmer still. Her blouse was an even paler blue, and just a trifle tight across her bust, to display her breasts without being in any way crude. Smart shoes, stockings, a neat little hat and leather gloves completed her uniform. She could have walked through Heathrow and nobody would have suspected for a minute that she was anything but a genuine air hostess, which made the display of her knickers far more arousing than had she been dressed for striptease.

The excuse she'd used to do it was wonderful too, if perhaps a little corny, suggesting that the services she provided might extend to rather more than wheeling the drinks trolley and calming those afraid of flying. When she'd started to talk about in-flight entertainment the more dirty-minded among the audience had begun to chuckle, but it was only when she turned around with a casual 'This, for instance' that they realised what they were in for. I'd known, as we'd agreed the whole act in advance, but it was still quite a shock.

Everybody was silent, waiting, and even I half expected her to simply tug her skirt down and go. She was looking directly at me, her gaze deliberately taunting, and, although she had hooked her thumbs into the back of her knickers, I still wasn't sure. I wagged a finger at her, hoping to remind her of her promise, although I knew it wouldn't make the slightest difference. She blew me a kiss, stuck her tongue out, pushed, and her knickers were down.

For one glorious moment the picture held, her upper body immaculate in her uniform, her lower body a vision of smart heels, taut nylons, the tangled cotton of her knickers and bare beautiful bottom. Her pussy lips were peeping out from between her thighs, pink and pouting, quite clearly moist with arousal, while her pose left her cheeks just far enough apart to hint at the wrinkled dun-brown star between. All of it showed, just as she'd promised, but the next instant she had covered herself up and was striding from the stage with a last flutter of her fingers.

The audience seemed to be spellbound, and didn't react until she had disappeared from view. Some began to clap, others to call for more, or simply to talk and laugh among themselves, full of amusement and excitement at what they'd seen. More than a few of them must have been feeling guilty, too, because when Violet kicked the door open there was a rustle of discontent, and one guy was making for the fire exit before he realised that she wasn't a real policewoman at all, but the next act.

She certainly looked the part, correctly dressed from her black-and-white check hatband to her regulation shoes and all points between. Only her walk gave her away, an arrogant strut that just oozed sex and power. As she made for the stage, I let my gaze run over the audience, taking in the expressions, both male and female: amusement, jealousy, desire, curiosity and, here and there, something not so very far from worship.

They were the ones whose eyes followed Violet's every move as she climbed up to the stage. She turned

3

around, and as she looked out over the audience she drew her truncheon, tapping it against her open palm. I could almost have believed her as she began her spiel, telling the audience off in no uncertain terms for watching strip shows. Even when she chose her victim it looked real, and it felt it for me, because I'd agreed to go up if nobody took the bait.

To my relief one man did, one of those who'd been staring. It must have taken guts, even if he was answering some deep fantasy, but once he had joined her on the stage there was no escape. She really put him through it, making him confess to a whole range of sins from being a Peeping Tom to 'intent to masturbate', which had half the audience laughing and the other half looking shocked.

She knew how to torment a man as well, making him apologise and then saying that was not enough, making him kneel and then saying that was not enough, making him kiss her shoes and then saying that was not enough. By then I could see him shaking from right across the room, and when she demanded that he go across her knee there was no resistance. Over he went, and he was spanked.

That was quite a sight, to see her in full police uniform, indistinguishable from the real thing, her face set in stern disapproval as she laid in, raining slaps on the seat of his trousers and telling him off at the same time. The audience lapped it up, or at least the great majoity of them did, and I couldn't help but smile, sure that there would be no shortage of stiff cocks and ready pussies, shortly to be put together. They'd remember, and they'd be back.

Laying on an all-uniform burlesque night had been a risk, what with licences and people with snooty attitudes and ditzy performers, but it had come off. All that remained was to get everyone out of the club and congratulate the staff and performers with a large drink. Half an hour later I was there, relaxing in an armchair in our waiting area with a glass of champagne in my hand as Paul slid the bolts home to shut out the world.

There were nine of us, myself and Paul in our monkey suits, the rest in uniform, even John if his chef's whites counted. I'd put my barmaid, Kiara, in a maid's outfit, and she'd been thoroughly enjoying herself. Even little Cathy on the door had insisted on dressing up in school uniform. Then there were the performers.

Vanity had been first on, looking amazingly smart in her US Navy dress whites. Her performance had been more comic than rude, but had left me wanting more, along with every other man in the audience and probably quite a few of the women.

Kitten was in a nurse's outfit, not one of those ridiculous plastic things but the real McCoy, which had made for a far more exciting show as she peeled slowly down to a tiny set of pink underwear that did very little to cover her glorious figure.

Angelique had adjusted her air-hostess uniform and looked so demure that, had I not known, I could never have believed that less than an hour before she'd been showing off her bare bottom for the entertainment of nearly three hundred men and women.

Violet was our policewoman. From what she'd said earlier I'd gathered she'd actually been in the force for a few years, which had made her performance all the more intriguing. I wanted to know more.

'So tell me,' I asked her, 'did you get into uniforms because you were in the police, or did you go into the police because you were into uniforms?'

'Neither, really,' she answered, 'but I did get thrown out of the police because I was into uniforms.'

'Oh yes?'

'Do tell,' Kitten put in, and everyone's attention turned to Violet.

She gave a meaningful nod towards the bar and Kiara scurried off to fetch another bottle. I did the honours, then settled back as Violet began to talk.

'I suppose I always had a bit of a thing for uniforms, but I'd never have thought of it that way. If you asked my sisters they'd tell you I was just plain bossy, because when we played at dressing up I always wanted to be the one in charge, and it just seemed right to dress the part. We all had nurses' uniforms, only mine was blue instead of white, and I wouldn't play unless I could be Sister.'

'Are you the eldest then?' John asked.

'No,' Violet answered. 'I'm in the middle. It's just my personality.'

'I'm surprised your big sister put up with that!' Vanity said with a laugh.

'Let Violet talk,' I urged.

I am bossy, I admit that, but that's just me. There was nothing sexual about it at all, not then. I just liked the way the uniform let me be in charge, but as I got older I slowly came to realise there was a link between that and my sexual feelings. There was nothing about anything like that in our sex-education lessons, and I thought I was weird, or even nuts, but I just couldn't help myself. I never told anybody, least of all the boys I went out with. Instead I started to look for excuses to dress up, so that I could enjoy it without giving myself away. School plays were always good, and whenever there was a fancy-dress party I'd really throw myself into it. I liked to be a pirate best, because I could stride around with my plastic sword and hit boys with it, and other girls. As long as it was a game you could always get away with it, although my parents and teachers used to get concerned. I suppose I was a little bitch, really, but still ...

What the hell, I don't suppose you lot mind, do you? I was thinking of the first time I ever came. There were these twins, Angela and David, who always stuck together, even when they were teenagers. Both of them were blonde, and she had hair right down to her knees. He was ... effeminate, I suppose you'd say, and both of them were quiet, but always eager to please. I liked people like that, because they'd do as they were told. At one of my parties – or it might even have been theirs – I was pretending to sword-fight with them, and when I won, inevitably, I made both of them kneel before me and kiss my shoes. That was all, but it really got to me, and that night I touched myself off under the covers, just thinking about the two of them kneeling at my feet, Angela with her beautiful hair spread out on the dirty ground and David looking up at me from soft blue eyes, as if he was really scared. Maybe he was.

My decision to join the police had nothing to do with all that, or at least not much, but I won't deny I was looking forward to wearing the uniform. Once I got into it, that was something else. I used to spend ages in front of the mirror, just soaking up the way I looked and imagining all sorts of scenarios, like arresting some really good-looking and arrogant young man and making him go down on me in return for being let off. That was always my thing, not the sort of subbie guys I get when I do my cabaret, but some real macho man who'd put up a fight but have to do it anyway, and end up tossing himself off while he licked me.

It was just fantasy, at first, and I tried so hard to keep it that way, believe me, but it didn't work. I even

7

remember the day I started to slip. When you're a policewoman and get called to a club or a party there's nearly always some joker to make a remark about you being a strip-o-gram. Generally I'd ignore them, or if they went too far I'd arrest them, but this time I just couldn't help myself. It was at a private party given by this guy who played for one of the Championship clubs. He really thought he was above the law, and when I turned up in response to a complaint about the noise he immediately came out with the old strip-o-gram joke.

I can see him now, in a silk shirt and these really tight trousers, lounging on a sofa with a girl either side of him, both of them giggling at my expense, and a lot of the other guests too. He called me 'darling' too, which I hate, so I just turned around to him and told him that if he didn't mind his language I'd have to spank him in front of his girlfriends. He was furious, and I do mean furious, so bad that me and my colleague had to warn him.

That was it, just the one line, but the way I'd put him down so easily and his helpless anger in response really aroused me. I tell you, I used to drive myself nuts imagining what might have happened when I was back at home with my rabbit vibrator for company. My favourite was for me to have done it to him, right there with all his silly little bimbos looking on, with his arse bare, and for him to get so turned on by it that when I'd finished he wouldn't be able to help himself. I used to think of how I'd make him go down on his knees to kiss my shoes, and hold him by the hair so that I could keep him under control while I very slowly lifted his head, dragging his lips up the insides of my calves, then my thighs, until I had his face trapped under my skirt so that he could lick me properly. Soon he'd be playing with his cock, because

8

he just couldn't help himself, and all the girls and his other guests would be staring in amazement, then laughing at him, or spanking him while he licked, or getting really disgusted when he came all over the floor. Not that it usually got that far, because just imagining his lips moving slowly up my legs was enough to get me there.

It might have been all right, even then, only the guy I was working with at the time thought it was really funny. He was one of the station jokers, and of course he told just about everybody else. They used to egg me on, and I've always been a sucker for the limelight, so I'd do it. Even then it probably wouldn't have mattered, or at worst I'd have got a ticking off from one of the sergeants, only I had to let it go too far. It was at the Christmas party, and some of the others were tormenting this young lad, telling him he had to go through with an initiation ceremony. Chris, the joker, started it, saying he'd have to kiss my feet or take a spanking. I was drunk and the new boy was really good-looking, so I took him over my knee and spanked him, right there in front of half my colleagues, in a pub.

He was pretty cross when he realised he'd been set up, but that didn't stop him hanging around me for the rest of the night, and I ended up taking him home. We were both drunk, and we just let ourselves go, or, rather, I did. He admitted he'd enjoyed being handled that way, and he was really turned on. Just kissing, I could feel his erection pressing against my leg. I told him he could have me if he did as I ordered and his answer was a whimper, which completely turned me on.

I made him strip, stark naked, but I kept my uniform on, not a button undone, not a hair out of place, and I played out the fantasy I'd brought myself

9

off to so many times. First I turned him over my knee, telling him he was a bad boy as I spanked him, and all the while his hard cock was pushing against my leg. I only stopped because I thought he was going to come on my uniform skirt, and by then he was willing to do anything. You know, I find that once I've spanked a man he'll do pretty much anything I ask.

With Danny – that was the recruit's name – I wanted to play out my fantasy, so I put him on his knees and stood over him. I could see myself in the mirror, my uniform just so and a naked man at my feet. I took him by the hair and made him kiss my shoes, watching while he did it, and higher, right up my legs, until his head was under my skirt. He was desperate for me, kissing me through the front of my knickers and tights and rubbing his face against me. It felt so good to have him trapped with his head under my uniform skirt, never mind what he was doing to me with his mouth.

I had to come, then and there, and I watched myself in the mirror as I used this man to bring me off. I didn't even bother to take my tights and knickers down but made him do it through the material, grinding myself hard into his face. He was pulling on his cock and he came at the same time as me, all over my shoes. I wanted more, so I made him lick it up, still holding him by the hair and laughing at him as his tongue flicked out to take up splashes of his own come from the shiny black surface of my police shoes. He did it too, almost eagerly, and even swallowed it down, which left me on a sadistic high like nothing I'd ever experienced before.

After that, there was no going back. Danny and I carried on for a couple of months, but he couldn't cope with what he liked to do. He was really into it, and when he was turned on he'd grovel at my feet and beg for permission to kiss my shoes, but he'd get ashamed of himself afterwards, especially around our colleagues, because, although we never told anyone what went on between us, they knew me and they could guess.

Eventually we split up, but by then I was completely addicted to having sex in my uniform. Do you know, Danny never saw me naked. I had to have more, but it wasn't easy to get, not the way I wanted it. Several of my colleagues were interested in me, but that was because they saw me as highly sexed, even as a challenge. I liked to dominate men so they wanted to dominate me in turn, or something like that. I accepted a couple of dates, but it never worked, and even with Danny it hadn't been completely real.

I wanted the man to feel he had no choice but to be under my control, and to get excited despite himself. The opportunity was there too, and if it hadn't been for nearly always working in pairs I'm sure I wouldn't have held out as long as I did. Unfortunately I got partnered with Chris, and that was fatal. He'd always tease me and, while I'd tell him to shut up and even hit him if nobody was looking, he made it harder than ever to resist temptation, and eventually I gave in.

There was a park on the edge of town, between the university and the closest thing we had to a sink estate. We'd been getting complaints about drug dealers, and our superintendent had set up an initiative to deal with it, which included foot patrols around the edge of the park. It didn't make much difference, because they could see us coming and the guys who made the deals never had anything on them anyway. We knew who the dealers were, and some of the students who were using, especially this one guy, Mac.

He was one of those kids who think they're cleverer than anyone else and better than anyone else, really cocksure. We knew full well what he was doing, but he knew we couldn't touch him, and he even used to make lippy remarks when he passed us in the park. That used to get to Chris, who didn't like to be on the receiving end, and, about the third or fourth time, he answered Mac back.

'Morning, coppers,' says Mac. 'Got any grass?'

'You know what kids like you need?' Chris answers back. 'A good spanking from time to time, and PC Chertsey here is just the one to give it to you.'

It was supposed to make Mac look small, but it didn't work. For about half a second he looked taken aback, then he turned around and stuck his arse out, right at us.

'Go on then, Miss,' he taunted. 'I like a bit of swish.'

I'd smacked him before I could stop myself, and it gave me such a kick I knew immediately that I'd have my rabbit down my knickers that night. Chris laughed, and Mac was demanding more, so I gave it to him, ten or twelve really hard swats, before I came to my senses and stopped. Mac just thought it was funny, and it left me embarrassed and angry and turned on all at once, but I couldn't get what I'd done out of my head. I was on edge all day, and that night I made myself come four times, wishing I still had my uniform on while I did it.

That was just the start. I couldn't keep away, and despite telling myself I was really out to make a bust I knew it was a lie. I suggested to Chris that the best way to deal with the drug problem was to watch for the couriers and then catch one of the students in possession, saying it would probably scare the others off. Maybe it would have worked, but that was not why I was doing it. I wanted Mac.

We changed our routine, walking through the park and then doubling back around the university buildings so that we could watch what was going on. It took a few days before we got lucky, or unlucky, and Mac appeared with another student. The courier was on a bike, but we weren't after him anyway, so, when the students split up, we followed and I took Mac, already knowing what I was going to do, because I just couldn't stop myself.

I followed him to his room in one of the accommodation blocks, more keyed up than I'd ever been, and constantly telling myself I wouldn't do it, although I knew I would. He hadn't seen me, and I caught him red-handed, rolling a joint on his desk. He hadn't even bothered to lock the door. Just to see him start when he realised it was me brought out the sadist in me, and got rid of any last chance that I'd back out.

For a moment the scene was frozen, with me standing in the doorway, eye to eye with Mac, who still had the piece of cannabis resin he'd been crumbling between his fingers. He knew I'd got him, but he was his usual lippy self.

'Ah, come on,' he says, 'you're not going to do me for a bit of weed, are you? Everybody does it.'

'Maybe,' I told him, 'but it's illegal. Still, if you promise not to do it again, maybe I could be lenient.'

'Yeah, yeah, I promise,' he answered, as cocky as hell.

'Stand up,' I told him.

'But you said . . .'

'Stand up. I'm not going to arrest you. I'm going to spank you.'

Just to get the words out of my mouth was like an electric shock. My skin was prickling all over and I

13

already felt hot between my legs, but – it's hard to describe – just having my uniform on made me feel as if I was in armour. He had stood up, but he was completely taken aback, his face working in surprise for quite a bit before he could get the words out.

'You're having a laugh!'

'No,' I told him, 'and, besides, I thought you said you liked a bit of swish?'

He didn't know what to say. His mouth opened and closed but no sound came out. As I closed the door behind me I knew I had him. The risk of other people hearing didn't occur to me, nothing like that. I wanted it, and I wanted it then and there. I sat down on his bed, struggling to look calm and absolutely raging inside. My legs were stuck out, making a lap, the same way I'd been used to spanking Danny when we were together, but Mac didn't move.

'Come on,' I urged. 'Get over my knee.'

'Yeah, but . . .'

'Get over my knee, now, and we'll say no more about it, or . . .'

'Yeah, OK. You're a fucking pervert, you know that?'

There was a whine in his voice, making me keener still as I patted my lap for him to get down.

'There's nothing perverted about spanking naughty little boys,' I told him. 'Now get into position, and you can undo your jeans first.'

He put his hands to his trousers but hesitated, his male pride fighting against what he knew it was sensible to do, and what he wanted to do deep down, I'm sure. Men always do, you know, if they can just get over their pride, and Mac was having real trouble. I could have soaked up that moment for ever, just watching as he struggled with his feelings, knowing perfectly well he was going to submit to my authority and like it, but fighting every inch of the way.

14

I didn't push him, but let him work it out for himself, and, sure enough, he flicked the button of his jeans open and pushed them down before getting across my knee. He'd been so full of himself before, but he was silent now, except for his breathing, and I could already feel the mass of his cock and balls pressing against my leg through my uniform skirt. Either he was very, very big or he was starting to get hard.

He was in red boxer shorts, quite loose, but showing off the outline of his firm, hard bum. I wanted to pull them down and touch him up while I spanked him, maybe humiliate him by milking his cock as he was punished, but I knew it was too early. Instead I took a firm grip around his waist and laid in, a good old-fashioned punishment spanking, hard and fast. He tried to keep quiet, but he couldn't and was soon making a right fuss, but that only turned me on all the more. Twice I had to threaten him to make him stay in position, but once his cheeks had started to heat up he was well and truly mine. I could feel his cock stirring too.

'You're going to do just what I tell you,' I told him. 'Exactly what I tell you, and no back chat, got it? First off, let's get your boxers down.'

He swore under his breath, and I knew he was still fighting his pride, but he didn't try to stop me as I tugged his boxer shorts down around his thighs. His skin was already quite red, and as I tugged his shorts out from between us I touched his cock, which was already stiff and very hot. That was more than I could resist, and I took hold, giving him a couple of sharp tugs before tucking him up between his belly and my uniform skirt. Then I went back to spanking him. In moments he'd begun to rub on my leg and I knew he was mine completely.

15

'If you spunk on my leg I'll make you lick it up,' I warned him.

There was no longer any possibility of pretending that what I was doing wasn't sexual, but that didn't mean I wasn't still in charge. He gave a little shiver as I spoke, but that didn't stop him rubbing and that didn't stop me spanking. I was imagining him doing it and me making him lick it up, with his tongue stuck out as he lapped up his own come from my uniform skirt, and that was too much for me.

'That's enough!' I told him after a last hard salvo of smacks. 'Now get on the floor.'

He obeyed, eager now, scrambling off my lap to lie down on the floor with his cock sticking up like a flagpole. I stood over him, bracing my feet to either side of his waist, so that he was looking up at me. He could see quite a lot of my legs, and maybe a hint of my nipples, which were achingly stiff, but that was all. It didn't seem to matter, because he was hammering at his cock with his eyes fixed to me, his pride broken and obviously going to come at any moment. I didn't want that.

'Leave your dirty little cock alone,' I told him. 'You're here for my pleasure. Do it!'

I lifted one foot and pressed the sole of my shoe down on his cock, which made him let go quickly. At that I sank down, kneeling across his face as I tugged up my uniform skirt and put his head under it. It was nearly summer by then, and I was in hold-ups, so he got a faceful of my knickers. I held him there, his head right up my skirt, and told him to lick. He tried to get his hands up, maybe to get me bare, maybe to touch me up, but I wasn't having it. I needed to be in full uniform.

'Do it through my knickers,' I told him, 'but you can touch my breasts, outside my uniform.'

He obeyed instantly, reaching up to feel the shape of my breasts through my uniform jacket while he nuzzled at my pussy, pushing my knickers in between my lips with his tongue. It was pure heaven, mounted on him with his head up my skirt as he licked me, completely in control, with his cock still rock-hard. That was what I'd wanted, a man helpless to me and to his own desire, a man who'd let himself be spanked on the bare and was now busily licking pussy, a man completely in thrall to my authority.

I came like that, one of the best orgasms of my life, grinding my pussy and bum into his face as he licked and squeezed at my breasts. He'd come too, without even touching himself, all over his belly and up the back of my uniform jacket, although I didn't realise at the time. That was what got me into trouble, because the little bastard didn't tell me and inevitably Chris wanted to know why I'd got spunk all over my jacket. He knew what I'd done, more or less, and tried to use it as leverage to get me into bed, but I wouldn't go for it, so he reported me.

That was that. I got slung out on my ear. As you can imagine, I had a bit of a bad time after that, and I was really down on myself for doing what I'd done with Mac. That didn't stop me wanting it, and by the time I'd picked myself up again and got a new job I'd realised that I really couldn't do without it. Like before, I tried to fight it, but it was too much. I like sex, and sex without my uniform on just wasn't the same. Even if I was in charge I could never get that amazing thrill of having total and real authority over a man. I kept thinking back to what I'd done with Mac, and nothing else seemed to satisfy.

After a couple of months I started doing strip-o-gram work, not just for the money, but in an effort to satisfy my needs and also to get back at the police in a funny sort of way. I always played it my way, with my uniform staying firmly on and the guy I was visiting getting cheek at the very least, maybe stripped off or even spanked. That made it awkward, because a typical party of lads want a naked girl, even if they do think it's hilarious when one of them gets dealt with. It wasn't satisfying my need either, because it was always too chaotic and never personal enough, although there were a few great moments when clients thought I was real.

That's why I switched to a burlesque act, so I'm more in control. It's good, but it's not what really gets me off. I'll tell you what really gets me off, and this is bad, very bad. I've still got the uniform, you see, because the day I got sacked I stormed out without even bothering to change, and because there was no way I could keep my flat up I moved back with my parents for a bit. If they ever demanded the uniform back, I didn't find out.

So I put on my uniform, under a coat, and with something from the agency to give me an excuse if I get challenged. I find some sexy young man and make him go down on me, all the while thinking I'm a real WPC. It doesn't always work, but most of the time they just don't think. They see a policewoman, so they obey her, and, when they think it's a choice of getting arrested or licking pussy, they lick pussy.

I know I shouldn't, but it's a compulsion. When I first did it I was telling myself it could never happen again, but it did, after nearly four months of trying to resist. I've done it three times now, successfully, and it's always been great. Do you want me to tell you? I'll tell you.

Just planning it is a thrill. I dress up in full uniform and go over how I'm going to get what I want, but I won't touch myself until I've finished. Then it's off to bed with my rabbit, still in uniform, of course. So, anyway, I'd decided that the safest way to do it was to stick to somewhere I knew and set up a failsafe in case any real police turned up. So I waited until one of the other strip-o-gram girls got a booking at this particular club with an alley behind, which made for a great excuse if I got caught, and somewhere to do the business.

I parked close by, in a quiet street, but it took real willpower to get out of the car and take my coat off. Just walking down the street was incredibly powerful, because people react differently to you when you're a policewoman, and of course I wasn't, I was impersonating one. I was terrified that somebody would ask for my help, or realise that I didn't have a radio, but they just ignored me.

The club was just off the High Street, but I knew there was a good chance of a patrol car being close, so I went down the back, to a cut-through at least some people would use. Most were in groups, and I stayed back in the shadows, watching, until most of them had dispersed. There were quite a few single men, but I found myself deciding against them for one reason or another, until I realised I was putting it off.

I had to force myself to make my choice, a blond guy, not too tall but well-built, bare-chested with his football shirt in one hand. He was good-looking, and he was quite drunk without being paralytic, just right. It took all the courage I had to step forwards and challenge him, but I did it, with my hand on the can of pepper spray in my pocket as I spoke to him, claiming he'd been seen in a fight earlier. He denied it, but we both knew he'd have done that anyway, and fortunately he had the sense to realise he was best off doing as he was told.

The look on his face when I suggested that there might be a way out of getting arrested was amazing, but he accepted it straight off. I'd been pretty sure he would, you see, because he was young, and good-looking, and arrogant, so he wasn't going to be surprised at a woman making a pass at him. Of course, he didn't realise what he was going to get. That took a little more, but the conversation between us was the sort of thing I'd been fantasising about for years. We'd barely got into a safe nook in a side alley between two rows of back gardens when he pulled his cock out.

'Down you go then, love,' he says, but I shook my head.

'Oh no,' I told him. 'You're the one who's going down.'

'You what?'

'I said, you're the one who's going down.'

'I don't do that, love.'

'You do now.'

'Nah, it's not right . . .'

'Oh, yes, it is, it's very right, for a dirty little boy who's got no choice. I'll tell you what, you can keep that out while you do it.'

I'd taken hold of his cock, gripping quite hard, and you should have seen the emotion working on his face as he looked at me. He wanted it, or at least he certainly wanted something, because he was getting stiff in my hand.

'It's that, or down the station,' I told him, exactly the threat I'd wanted to deliver so often.

'OK, OK, only . . .'

'Get down on your knees.'

I put my back to the fence and pushed him down by his head. He went, kneeling in the mud at my feet, his face looking up at me, a pale oval in the

20

half-darkness, ashamed and excited all at once. I tugged my skirt up and took him by the hair, pulling his face in between my thighs as I pushed them out. I was in stockings under my uniform, stockings and tight black knickers, which he was trying to pull down.

'Uh, uh,' I ordered, 'no, you don't. Do it through them.'

His face was right against my pussy, and I'd begun to rub myself on him, but he'd already given in, nuzzling me with his lips and pushing my knickers into my slit with his tongue, right onto my clit.

'Right there, that's a good boy,' I told him, 'and don't stop until I say. You can wank your cock too.'

He didn't need telling, pulling at himself as he licked me, his excitement high enough for him to get over his shame. I had him, and I relaxed into it, just utter bliss, to think what I'd done, what a risk I was taking, and how he felt, an arrogant young man on his knees in the mud as he licked a policewoman through her knickers and pulled on his cock.

Now he was behaving himself I could really let go, with my eyes closed as I stroked my uniform, touching my raised skirt with the bump of his head underneath it, the shape of my jacket over my hips and waist and breasts. I didn't need light to picture myself, because I knew exactly how I looked in police uniform, every detail of jacket and skirt and blouse just so, only now with his head up my skirt as he wanked at his cock.

He got there first, on the ground between my feet, and he was going to stop, but I took him firmly by the head and held him in place, making him finish me off. That must have been so shameful, with the come dribbling down his hand because he hadn't been able to hold back when he was the one being made to give pleasure with his mouth. That was what I came over,

21

imagining his humiliation at being forced to lick a policewoman out and ending up tossing himself off in the mud before she'd even got there.

I felt really light-headed afterwards, once he'd run for it, and I walked back to the car in a daze. It was only when I'd got home and given myself a second orgasm with my rabbit that the risks I'd taken really hit home. I couldn't stop shaking, and I kept thinking of all the things that might have gone wrong, from getting arrested to him turning on me. It was horrible, like a bad trip, but, even as I lay shivering in my bed with every nightmare scenario you can imagine running through my head, there was still a thrill, deep down. All night and all the next day I was the same, cursing myself for being such an idiot and promising I'd never ever do it again, but within days the urge had started to grow once more.

You can't understand it unless you've been there. After a couple of weeks I knew I had to do it again. The need had become a physical ache and the pleasure of coming over my memories was fading. I held off as long as I could, but it was making me a nervous wreck and eventually I gave in and began to plan another excursion.

The crucial thing was that the man had to believe it was real, but he needed to be good-looking too, and a bit arrogant. I didn't want a pushover, but I knew I couldn't risk anyone too bolshie. Mac had been good, and students seemed safer than the lads from the town, so I started to think about some of the more athletic types from the university. The far side of the campus was open country, and I quickly discovered that quite a few of them went running, often early in the morning and nearly always alone. It seemed perfect, but I needed an excuse to get one under my thumb.

My first thought was to pretend to catch one for trespass, because while there were two long footpaths running parallel it was hard to get from one to the other without crossing private land, which also meant lots of places for me to have my wicked way with only a minimal risk of getting caught. I tried that twice, going through all the stress of preparing myself, only to have the first one make a run for it and the second give me a long lecture on the right to roam.

That put me off for a while, and I nearly abandoned the plan, but the need was still there. I decided it would be better to make up an incident, the way I had before, and something relatively serious. Like every time, it took all my courage to go out there and actually stop somebody, but the guy I chose was too beautiful to ignore. He was tall, with a very aristocratic face, the sort I always associate with pictures of pilots from the Battle of Britain, and the last person you'd expect to get into a road-rage incident, which is what I accused him of. Of course he denied it, but I insisted he fitted the description I'd been given and told him he'd have to come down to the police station.

He agreed, but he was very different from the lad in town, trying to explain himself and assuring me of his innocence. That made it even harder to proposition him, and when I did I could see the doubt in his eyes. I'm still not sure exactly what he was thinking, but he accepted, and let me lead him in among the trees, where I told him he was going to have to lick me. He was smiling as he agreed, which again took a bit of the gloss off it, so I made him lie down and told him to take his cock out.

'Yes, Ma'am,' he answered, which was good, but there was no shame in his face.

23

'Now wank yourself hard,' I ordered.

'How about a little peep?' he asked.

'You'll do as you're told,' I insisted, and stayed as I was, my feet braced either side of his legs as he got himself erect, his eyes feasting on the shape of my breasts under my uniform jacket.

He was hard in moments, obviously enjoying my body, but I wanted to humiliate him.

'I'm going to sit on your face,' I told him. 'How about that?'

His answer was an urgent nod, not what I'd expected at all, but I hadn't come that far to back out. I straddled his head and tugged up my uniform skirt, all the while with him staring up at me. He'd stuck his tongue out even as I began to squat down, and the moment I got his head under my skirt and my knickers in his face he was licking. It did feel good, sitting on a beautiful young student's face in my full uniform, but he had none of the reluctance or helpless arousal I wanted, far from it. He was wanking furiously as he licked, and it wasn't his first time. The lad in town had been clumsy, licking at me like a dog trying to lap up water, but not this one. He kept teasing me, licking my thighs between my stocking tops and my pussy, and trying to get his tongue in around the edge of my knickers. I told him to behave himself and moved forwards a little so that my bum was in his face in an effort to punish him. He just stuck his tongue further out, pushing my knickers into my slit, and at that moment he came, all over my back.

I made him finish, calling him a dirty little boy and a male tart and anything else I could think of as I ground my pussy into his face, but he lapped it all up, literally. It was good when I came, but nothing like as intense as the one before, and afterwards the

24

cheeky sod suggested we meet up again. I accepted, even though it wasn't ideal, hoping that our arrangement would be enough to satisfy my lust. It wasn't, and even though I met him another three times it was never as good as it might have been.

What it did do was lead me on to the third encounter, which really had everything. In order to meet up with Robin, my student, I would park my car at the edge of a wood where a lot of people went to walk their dogs. The council had made a sort of crude car park, with an iron gateway to stop caravans and lorries getting in, and big chunks of concrete so that nobody could drive into the wood itself. It was always much too busy for my purposes, even quite early in the morning, with people out walking their dogs before work, but the third time I met Robin I made a discovery.

It was late afternoon, and I'd just spent a happy half-hour sitting on his face in a little glade well into the woods. He still thought I was a genuine WPC, but that was as far as the pretence went. He'd had my knickers off, and my jacket and blouse open at the front so he could play with my tits, which was nice but just didn't give me that special thrill. I was wondering what I could do about the situation as I walked back, but as I got near the car park I realised I wasn't the only one parked there.

It was already getting dark, but I could see that one of the cars was white and thought it might be a patrol car, so I moved forwards cautiously. I'd realised it wasn't a police car at all but just a couple having a quickie in the back seat, when I saw the man among the bushes. He hadn't noticed me, because all his attention was on the car, and no surprise. The car guy had his girlfriend's top up and was stroking her tits, and the guy in the bushes was a Peeping Tom, and then some. He had his cock out, wanking over them, and after a few seconds of staring at this scene I realised that the couple were deliberately showing off.

I knew what I wanted to do on the spot, and if the Peeping Tom had been attractive I'd have had him then and there. He wasn't, so I tried to back away, but he heard me and turned around. The expression on his face when he saw a policewoman standing maybe ten feet behind him was something else, and he panicked, trying to stuff his erect cock back in his fly and run at the same time, which must be the funniest sight I've ever seen. I let him go, which must have come as a relief, but of course I wouldn't have known what to do with him if I had caught him.

That evening it was rabbit time with a vengeance. I came five times, just thinking about the possibilities the situation had offered. It was tailor-made for me, because I could stay back in the bushes and pick and choose my men, who'd be caught red-handed doing something deeply shameful and so would be sure to comply. If any real police turned up I could easily melt into the woods.

I was a lot less apprehensive this time, but I didn't want to rush it, so made several visits to the woods first, both at night and during the day. Soon I'd learnt everything I needed to know, where all the little paths led and which were the best times. Early evening, just after it got dark, was ideal, because it was quite a popular place and after chucking-out time there might be three or four cars and maybe as many as ten men watching. 'Dogging', it's called, and they even have internet sites devoted to it, which helped me evolve my strategy.

My first three outings were failures, because none of the men I saw appealed to me, and I realised I had a problem. The couples who came to show off were often quite attractive, but the Peeping Toms were basically a bunch of dirty old men. It wasn't impossible, though, because I knew that all I had to do was step out into the open and they'd all run for it, but if a couple were half-naked in the back seat they were going nowhere.

The fourth time I went out the same couple I'd seen on my first visit were there. They seemed to be waiting, she doing her make-up in the rear-view mirror, he looking out at the woods. I knew there was a system of signals, involving flashing headlights, which they did occasionally, and after a while there was an answering flash from the bushes opposite me. At that they climbed into the back, still with the interior light on. He was eager, immediately tugging up her top and bra to show off her tits, while she was nervous but obviously excited.

I watched, enjoying the show, but nothing like as much as I was enjoying what I hoped would come later. He was attractive in a rather flash way, with slicked-back black hair and gold rings on three fingers. She was petite and quite delicate, with dyed blonde hair and small breasts. I'm not a lesbian or anything, but the thought of making her watch while I dominated her man was making me shake with desire. Maybe that's wrong, but I had to so badly that I stepped out from the bushes without further thought.

The Peeping Tom must have seen me first, because there was a rustle in the bushes where he'd been, but the couple probably couldn't see anything outside the lit interior of the car and I came right up to their window without being seen. When I tapped on the glass they both started and looked around. Presumably they were expecting some unusually pushy dirty old man, because they didn't look worried until they saw my uniform. When they did, they looked scared: one of the most delicious moments of my life.

'Out, both of you,' I ordered.

She was bright red in the face as she struggled to cover herself up, and he wasn't much better, both of them stammering apologies and excuses as they climbed out of the car. I was so aroused it took an effort to go into my routine instead of just pushing him down and making him do me in front of her, but I managed it, putting the fear of God into them before offering an alternative. He looked shocked, and I thought she was going to cry, but they followed me into the woods meekly enough.

I'd chosen my place carefully, a little clearing where a tree had fallen, shielding us from the car park and road. Using my torch to make a puddle of light, I sat down on the trunk of the tree and beckoned him forwards. She was staring, her mouth slightly open, her eyes wide, and her nipples as stiff as corks under her top where she'd failed to get her bra on properly. If she'd been angry or had broken down I'd have stopped, but she was showing that perfect mixture of shame and desire I like so much. So was he, and with a touch of aggression in his eyes, so I reminded him of his choices one more time, then pointed at the ground.

'Come on. Get down.'

He glanced at her. She made a face, then spoke.

'You'd better do it, Tony.'

For one instant our eyes met, and maybe there was a touch of conspiracy in her look, maybe not. He came forwards though, reluctantly, his face hard as he got down on his knees, but his uncertainty showing in his eyes. I set my knees apart and lifted the hem of my uniform skirt, making a dark cavity into which he was to insert his head.

'I imagine you know what to do?' I asked him.

He nodded and shuffled forwards on his knees. I took his head and pulled him in, his face pressed to the crotch of my knickers, the way I like best.

'Lick me through them,' I ordered.

He got straight down to business, drawing a little sob from her to see her precious boyfriend made to lick a policewoman's pussy while she watched. The sense of power as he nuzzled and kissed me through my knickers was as good as anything that had gone before, maybe better, while making her watch added a whole new dimension – yet I still wanted more.

'Get your cock out,' I instructed. 'You can toss off while you do it, and you, pull your top up again.'

She obeyed straight away, her face a picture of shame and excitement as she lifted her top over her tiny breasts, but he was stubborn.

'Come on,' I urged. 'Your girlfriend's tits are out, so get wanking, or I'll spank you in front of her.'

That got him. His cock was out of his fly in seconds and his reluctance had been a lie, because he was already hard. The moment it was out he was pulling at himself, and she was staring wide-eyed. Her hand had gone to the V between her legs, though, pressing her pussy through her jeans, unconsciously I think, and I couldn't help but taunt her.

'You're turned on, aren't you? You're turned on watching Tony lick me, aren't you? Why don't you play with yourself then, you little slut?'

She shook her head and took her hand away from her pussy, but she was still watching, her eyes flicking between the bulge of his head beneath my uniform skirt and the pale shape where his cock stuck out beneath his belly as he wanked. I laughed at the state she was in and began to show off, rubbing his face into my pussy and stroking my breasts through my uniform jacket, all the while looking right into her eyes.

'Do it,' I urged, 'or get down next to him and milk his cock for him. I bet you like to do that, you dirty little bitch.'

Again she shook her head, but I wasn't having it.

'Do it, or I spank him!' I snapped, and Tony was urgently nodding his head and making muffled noises through his mouthful of knickers and pussy.

'You're evil, you know that?' she told me, but she was already getting to her knees.

'I know,' I told her, because I could already feel my orgasm rising up and I just didn't care any more, 'but for that you can do yourself too.'

She gave me what was supposed to be a dirty look as her hands went to the button of her jeans, but there was no mistaking the lust in her eyes. Down came her jeans and knickers, and I was laughing as her little round bum and shaved pussy lips came bare. She took his cock in one hand, the other slipped between her thighs, and that was too much for me. There she was, kneeling in the mud and leaves with everything that matters on show, masturbating as she milked her boyfriend onto the ground, and him with his head up my police skirt, licking pussy in front of her.

I came so hard I almost fainted, but I kept my grip on the back of his head and my eyes locked to hers until my vision began to swim. They didn't stop either, but finished themselves off right there in front of me, him in her hand and her under her own fingers, simply unable to stop themselves, for all their shame in what I'd made them do to me.

Two

I couldn't help wondering if Violet was exaggerating, or even making it up completely, but it wasn't the time to challenge her. I could see she had turned herself on, and the others. Kiara in particular was full of nervous excitement, fidgeting in her lap with her tiny maid's skirt pushed so far up that almost the full length of her smooth stocking-clad thighs showed, along with a hint of tanned flesh and frilly white panties between.

'Would you like to have done that yourself, Kiara?' I asked.

She shook her head, looking embarrassed, and then began to speak.

'Not what Violet did, no, but I, maybe, wouldn't have minded being on the other end, like the girl in the car.'

'Oh yes?' Violet asked. 'Would you have done what she did?'

Kiara nodded and for a moment her golden skin grew darker as the blood went to her face.

'I like the idea, anyway,' she said, 'especially of being taken charge of, and doing dirty things because I'm told to, or because it goes with the way I'm dressed.'

'Like bending down so your knickers showed while you were serving this evening?' John laughed.

'Yes,' Kiara answered, her voice surprisingly serious and a little defensive. 'That's how you wanted me to behave, wasn't it?'

'Yes, of course,' I assured her. 'You were great.'

'Thank you,' she said, 'and it's true, isn't it? If I'm in a tiny little skirt and frilly knickers, it's so I can show off?'

'Yes,' John admitted.

'There we are then,' Kiara went on, 'and I do like it, but it's not so much showing off as being made to show off. That's why I like to be put in uniform, and I don't know why, but people always seem to want to dress me up anyway, as if I was a doll or something.'

'That's just men for you,' Kitten put in. 'Perverts, the lot of them.'

'So Richard put me in a maid's uniform,' Kiara went on, throwing me a look of mock disapproval, 'just so everybody gets to see my knickers.'

As she spoke she had tugged down the hem of her skirt, covering a little more of her thighs, but in doing so providing a clear flash of the lacy white triangle where her panties covered her sex. She smiled, clearly aware of what she was doing but still doubtful as she went on.

'Not that I mind, and it's not as if it was the first time either. The last place I worked was worse than here, and my ex-boyfriend Giles was a uniform fiend.'

'That's lucky, I had to make my own,' Cathy cut in, and would have continued but I raised a hand.

'You'll get your turn. I want to hear about Kiara's ex, and the place she worked, what was it called, Oh-La-La?'

That's right, Oh-La-La. It's a bit of a clip joint, really, and a lot of the men who go there are creeps, but the other girls were nice and I did like being put in uniform. Then there was the house mother, but I'll come back to her.

The design of our maids' uniforms was even more revealing than this one. They were in satin, with a tight waist and a bodice so low that if you were at all big you were in serious danger of falling out, and a skirt so short that you only had to bend a tiny bit to have your knickers showing. That was the idea, of course, and when we served we had to do it a special way. We had to put our feet together and keep our legs straight, then bend at the waist and hold the pose while we took the drinks off the tray and put them down on the table. Of course that meant the full length of our legs and the seat of our knickers would be on show behind, and a lot of cleavage at the front. With a tray in your hands there wasn't a lot you could do to protect yourself either, and it was risky, because sometimes the men used to pop our tits out or pinch our bums, even pull our knickers down at the back. Of course you could get them thrown out for that, but that didn't help with the embarrassment of having your tits flopped out in front of a load of dirty old men or your bum bared to the entire club.

Of course I pretended I hated it, and I did in a sense. At least, I hated the men for it, but I loved the feeling of being put in a uniform which meant I had to show off and was constantly at risk of exposure. I suppose that wouldn't make sense to a lot of people, but you don't have to like someone for them to turn you on. No way would I ever have gone with any of the men, not for anything, but one time after I'd had my tits popped out . . . But I'll tell you.

Our uniforms all looked the same, but they were different colours, so when the girls lined up at the beginning of the evening we were like a rainbow. Because I'm quite dark I'd been given a scarlet one,

33

but it was a bit small for me, so Bea, that's the house mother, said she'd make an alteration when she had time, but not then. I felt horribly conspicuous with my tits bulging halfway out of the top of my uniform, and I was sure they'd fall out every time I bent down to serve. They stayed in, fortunately, but it was the same the next night, with Bea fussing over one of her favourites and ignoring me completely.

That went on for most of my first week, by which time I'd realised that they weren't actually going to fall out, at least not of their own accord. I suppose I was a bit naïve, and what with the bouncers there and everything I didn't think any of the men would break the club rule, which was strictly 'no touching'. So you can imagine my shock when I bent to serve at this table of Japanese businessmen and one of them suddenly grabs my tits and pops them both out of my uniform.

He took me completely by surprise. One moment I'd been in my serving pose, balanced on my heels with my bum stuck in the air and my frillies on show but nothing worse, and the next I'm tits-out topless with one dangling in a glass of beer I'm supposed to be serving to them. I screamed and jumped up, which upset the beer into their laps, and they started yelling at me, as if it was my fault.

I was still trying to get my tits back in when a bouncer came over, and one of them was all wet and slippery with beer so I couldn't get it in the cup properly, and do you know what those bastards did? They denied grabbing me and made out that I'd fallen out of my dress because I was too big for it. I tried to explain what had really happened, but they just started dishing out money. In the end they were allowed to stay and I was the one who got told off, both by Bea and my manager, before being made to apologise to the men.

You can imagine how that made me feel, about the size of a mouse, and about as significant. I ran into the changing room at the back, almost in tears, but as I tidied myself up the thought of what had been done to me kept going around and around in my head. I could feel myself getting hotter, and I knew why after the way my ex had treated me, but I didn't want to admit to myself that I could get turned on by having some bastard pop my tits out of my uniform in public.

It was no good, though. One whole side of the room was mirrored, and I could see myself in my scarlet uniform with its tiny skirt leaving my legs bare and my flesh bulging out around the top of my bodice. I looked like what I was, a sex toy for a load of dirty old men. At least that's how I felt, and how I wanted to feel, and I couldn't help myself. I started to show off in front of the mirror, standing in my serving pose but with my back slightly turned, so that I could see the way my scarlet high heels made my legs tense and how my frillies came on show as I bent forwards. It made me look so rude, and so available, as if being in my tarty little uniform marked me as ready for sex.

Next I turned face-on to watch the way my breasts lolled forwards to show my cleavage in the same position, just the way I'd been made to show them off to so many men. Only it had gone further. I'd had them popped out and left dangling bare in front of the Japanese businessmen. The one who'd done it had squeezed them, and all of them had had a good eyeful, as well as another twenty or thirty men at nearby tables, but it was me who'd been made to apologise to them.

That thought hurt so much, and turned me on so much, that before I knew it I'd popped them back out, staring at myself in the same sexy, silly pose I'd been in for the businessmen: tits out of my uniform in the middle of the club, with their greedy little eyes drinking in my flesh. I imagined how it would have been if they'd gone further, felt me up, maybe held me down and taken my knickers off so I had to work with my pussy bare at the front and my bum showing every time I bent over.

I just couldn't stop myself, staring at my image in the mirror, the little scarlet waitress's uniform with my bare breasts and frilly knickers . . . and I stuck my hand down the front. As I played with myself I was thinking of how they'd used me and how I'd been made to apologise for my own abuse, how being in my uniform made me into a sex toy, how awful it had felt to have my tits popped out, and how much worse it would feel to have my knickers pulled off and my pussy filled up from behind by a laughing Japanese businessman while his friends held me down over the table.

So that was it, but I never admitted what I'd done, or how being in my uniform made me feel, not to the other girls, and certainly not to the men. It's weird, because in a club like that you have layer after layer of pretence. We had to pretend to the men that we were basically a bunch of brainless little tarts whose sole ambition was to serve them and show off our bodies for their amusement, although of course everybody knew that our real job was to get as much money out of them as possible. Then there was the way we behaved among ourselves, telling each other how awful the men were and making up names for the regulars like Baldy and Fats, but actually some of them were OK. I got told off by Bea once for having a long conversation with this guy we used to call Mr Blobby, just about Minehead, where we'd both been on holiday. Because he was nice to me I hated having to show off for him, if that makes any sense at all. It was the bastards who made me feel excited, although I'd have happily kicked most of them in the balls.

The same thing happened a few times after that, but it was never as powerful as the first time. I was on the lookout for it, and Bea finally got around to adjusting my uniform, so it wasn't so easy to do me. She started to be nice to me too, which was scary, because I'd worked out what that meant. Her job was to look after the girls, but she was always playing favourites and always seemed to pick on the new girls. Our turnover was pretty high, as you can imagine in a place like that, and generally somebody would leave or somebody new would turn up every couple of weeks.

Her big favourite had been a girl called Alice, who was either just a natural flirt or as hard as nails, I never worked out which. She was always smiling, and would do her serving pose perfectly, with her back pulled in so her uniform skirt would go up as far as possible and make her bum look big and round. When we'd talk about the men she'd usually just shrug, as if it was no big deal to have her bum pinched or her thighs slapped. Maybe it wasn't, not compared with what Bea was doing to her.

I'd guessed something was going on, but I didn't know what. Sometimes they'd leave together, and we'd guessed they were going to bed together, but I assumed they'd just take turns to lick each other. One or two of the more worldly girls claimed that Bea had a strap-on, and it was obvious that if so she would be the one doing the fucking and Alice would be the one getting fucked, but I thought they were just being dirty.

Alice was working to pay her way through college, like a lot of the girls, and once her final exams were over she left. Bea was in a foul mood for days, then started to pay attention to one of her other favourites, Danielle, until she suddenly left. A few days later I was about to go out when she came up behind me and told me to straighten up. I wasn't even sure what she meant but, before I realised, she had taken hold of my frilly knickers at the back and tugged them a little to the side and tighter up my bum. She then sent me out of the room with a little slap under my cheeks.

I was blushing as I went out, partly because she'd pulled my knickers up so tight that I had a lot more cheek showing out of my leg holes than usual, and partly because I could still feel a tingling sensation where she'd slapped me. She was watching me too, which wasn't unusual as she always kept an eye on us while we were working, but this time nearly all her attention seemed to be on me. It made me feel more self-conscious than ever while I served, especially when I had to adopt the position, and a lot of men made remarks about how much cheek I was showing.

Nobody molested me, much, but by the end of that evening I'd got that helpless feeling back again, making me thoroughly ashamed of myself, but also wishing I had a chance to stay in my uniform long enough to bring myself off in front of the mirror again. That wasn't going to happen, because we had to leave everything there for cleaning, and so we didn't nick anything. But I was quite hopeful when Bea singled me out to collect the glasses from the balcony area after closing time. That meant I'd be last out, unless I hurried, and if I took my time there was a fair chance I'd be able to do the dirty deed.

So I took my time and, sure enough, once I got into the changing room most of the other girls were already dressed. Unfortunately Bea was there, sitting on the chair by the door where she always watched us get ready. She began to talk to me, and obviously wasn't going to go away, so I started to undress, kicking off my heels and quickly pushing my knickers down, very conscious of her watching. I was going to shower, and of course that meant stripping off all the way, but the moment my knickers were off Bea spoke up again.

'Your posture isn't all that good, Kiara.'

'Oh, sorry.'

'You ought to practise more. Show me.'

'Um . . . OK.'

I reached for my knickers. I was embarrassed at the thought of being made to do my poses in front of her, on my own, even with them on, but bare was worse by far. Unfortunately she knew that, and it was exactly what she wanted.

'Don't bother with those. Do you think it matters, in front of me?'

Of course it mattered, and she knew it, but I couldn't help myself. I should have told her where to go, and part of me wanted to, but I hesitated just too long.

'Put your shoes back on and do it,' she instructed.

I obeyed. I don't know why, because I was burning with embarrassment and already wondering how it would feel to be taken to bed by her, but I couldn't stop myself. At the moment she had told me to put my heels on it had become erotic, and she knew it. That didn't stop us pretending I really needed to improve my posture. I slipped my feet into my shoes and put them together, keeping my legs straight and bending from the waist as we were taught to do.

As the skirt of my waitress uniform lifted I knew exactly what I was showing, because I could see in the mirror: not the seat of my frillies, but my bare bottom, with my pussy lips sticking out between my thighs. She could see too, not straight on, but in the reflection, and she left me like that for a long time, her eyes caressing my body, before she spoke.

'You need to pull your back in more, the way Alice used to do it.'

I knew exactly what she meant, and the consequences, but I did it anyway, blushing like anything as I made a swan's neck of my back. I was looking around, I couldn't help it, and the feeling as I saw myself had me shaking. My uniform skirt had come up higher still, to show off almost the whole of my bum, which looked big and round. My pussy lips were sticking right out, and I could see I was wet, but worst of all, my cheeks had come apart and my bumhole was showing to her.

'Better,' she said. 'Stay like that, and stop looking at yourself.'

Again I couldn't stop myself obeying, for all my trembling and the awful bubble of shame and apprehension in my throat. She stood up, came close and walked around me, her eyes feasting on my body. I thought she was going to pop my tits out, but she seemed content with them in my bodice and simply made a small adjustment to the front of my uniform so that they hung better inside, with her thumbs pressed to my flesh less than an inch from my nipples. I was hard, and she must have seen, but she carried on, walking around behind me.

I knew what she could see, which was making the muscles of my legs and bum twitch, but I didn't dare look around. I was sure she'd touch me, and not sure I could cope at all, but what she did was lift my uniform skirt right up over my back to leave the whole of my bottom showing, which threw me completely.

'You have a nice bottom,' she said, 'but you must learn to show it off properly. Stick it out. Wiggle it a bit. That's what the men like.'

'Yes, I know,' I told her, although my words came out as a whisper.

'Then why don't you do it?' she asked.

'I . . . I'm embarrassed to,' I admitted.

She just grunted, then suddenly slapped my bottom, not hard, really just the same little pat she used to send the girls out at the beginning of the evening, but it made me jump. She gave a nasty little laugh and did it again, then spoke.

'I think maybe you'd benefit from a good spanking.'

'A spanking? What for? I haven't done anything wrong!'

It was the most stupid thing to say, because of course she had no right to spank me at all, whether I'd done anything wrong or not, but I suppose I just reacted instinctively. She'd begun to slap my bottom anyway, no harder than before, but I didn't stop her and she seemed to take that for acceptance. Maybe it was, I really don't know.

She gave me about ten little pats, then took hold of my wrist and before I knew it I'd been pulled over to her chair and put across her knee. That got my attention, and I was squealing and protesting like anything as she turned my uniform skirt back up again to get my bottom bare, but she took no notice at all, just laying into my bum with one great big hand and holding me down with the other.

It hurt like anything, and I was squealing like a pig and kicking my legs about, struggling so hard my tits fell out of my uniform, which really made her laugh. She kept at it, though, laughing and telling me not to be such a big baby as she smacked my bum and

41

thighs. I could see myself in the mirror too, and a fine sight I looked, with my uniform skirt turned up at the back and tits hanging out at the front, my legs kicking up and down and my bum all red.

I don't know how long she kept me over her knee, but it seemed like forever, with my poor bottom getting hotter and hotter, and my pussy too. I'd never been spanked before, and it was hideously embarrassing to find that it made me wet between my legs, but there was nothing I could do. I was turned on, and she knew it, so that when she finally stopped there was no question of what was going to happen. The spanking had given me the most amazing glowing feeling in my bum, more hot than painful, and the urge to stick it out and get my legs apart was huge.

If she'd had her strap-on dildo she could have fucked me, right there on the changing-room floor, and at that moment I'd have taken it and loved it. What I got was her pussy in my face, kneeling on the floor with my uniform tugged up and down, tits-out topless and bare red bum stuck out behind as I brought her off with my tongue. I'd never done that before either, so in the space of a few minutes I'd been spanked and made to lick pussy for the first time in my life. She made me come too, by holding me down across her lap and frigging me off while she spanked me.

After that it was like she owned me. She'd give me all the best jobs and make sure I didn't have to serve the real arseholes, but she'd keep me in after work and make me pose for her, or serve her drinks, both of which usually ended with a spanking and maybe oral sex. After about a week she took me to bed, but for some reason that was easier to take than the rest of it, because she treated me like a person instead of a doll. Not that I minded being made to pose so much, or even the spankings, which did turn me on, but what made it impossible to take was the way the other girls reacted.

We'd all been friends, and we were always talking to each other and going out together, because what we did wasn't something it was easy to share with outsiders. What I hadn't realised was just how much we relied on each other for our strength, and once I was Bea's favourite I wasn't one of the girls any more. They ignored me most of the time, and a few were really spiteful, which hurt, but the worst part of it was feeling as if I was alone. So I quit and moved on here, which is far better, believe me, but I do miss having to dress up, which is why I had so much fun tonight.

It's quite a nice memory now, all that, but I don't think I could have taken it at all if it hadn't been for my Giles – that's my ex. He was the one who taught me how it feels to be made into a dolly for somebody else's kicks, and the one who taught me to enjoy it. But he always had difficulty getting hard. I remember how I used to sit for ages parked up somewhere in the front of his car with my tits out while I pulled up and down on his cock, and I think I'd have given up on him if anyone else I fancied had shown an interest. But they didn't.

Then this one time we were invited to a fancy-dress party by a friend of mine who really reckoned herself and had rich parents too. I knew everyone would be putting in a big effort, so I went as a sort of girlie Pierrot, in full black-and-white costume and make-up, with a curly gold wig and gold slippers. The skirt was cute, like a ballet skirt only in black-and-white harlequin with gauze underneath to support it, and I had these little gold shorts on underneath in case anyone saw my knickers.

I can't remember what Giles came as, except that his costume was mostly black, but I do remember how horny he was, right from the start. He was trying to kiss me and touch my tits before we'd even got there, and all through the party he was trying to get me alone. I let him in the end, and we did it on my friend's mum and dad's bed. I'd never seen him like it before. He couldn't keep his hands off me, but he didn't want me to undress, only to take my shorts down so he could get in, and he was rock-hard even before I got him out of his trousers.

He gave it to me really hard too, with me on my knees and my shorts down at the back, and it was more like he was trying to devour me than make love to me. It was hot, though, and it left me feeling really good, not just satisfied, but really wanted too. It was only the next time we went out that I realised it wasn't me he wanted at all, because he was just like he'd been before, limp. He wanted me to dress up again, only of course I'd taken my Pierrot back to the shop.

I was a bit pissed off about it, but it's in my nature to always try and oblige, so I put on my school uniform when he asked, and he managed to have me, but it was nothing like the time before. Then there was the plastic sexy nurse outfit he bought me one time, but it was just tacky. I hated it, but at least he could get hard, and I used to bend over my bed so my bum showed under the skirt while he wanked himself up. He always used to have me from behind too, because that way he could see that I was dressed up.

It was after being fucked in that stupid nurse's outfit about ten times that I decided that, if he couldn't get it up without me as a doll, then I might as well dress up in something I liked. I got a ballet outfit first, in white with the classic flared skirt and tights underneath, but that didn't do much for him unless I was plastered in make-up, which was when I realised that what he really wanted wasn't a human girl at all but a sort of living doll he could dress up however he liked.

I suppose a psychiatrist would say he had difficulty relating to real people, and maybe that's the way it was, but I just remember the effect I had on him with my ballet outfit on and my face painted in the same style as my Pierrot make-up. I didn't even have to pose for him or wank him hard. He pushed me down over the bed, tore my tights open to get at me and stuffed it up from behind. I wasn't even properly ready and it hurt a bit at first but, believe me, that's better than pulling on a limp cock for half an hour with your tits on show for any dirty old men who happen to be passing.

I felt quite sexy in my ballet outfit, and would happily have stuck with that, despite the cost in tights, but he wasn't satisfied. He wanted my costume more elaborate and for me to wear more make-up, until he'd have me done up like a giant china doll, with frills all over and red patches on my cheeks and the whole works. I tried to accommodate him, but finally rebelled when he wanted to do me up as a girl golliwog.

There was a brief lull after that, and it was back to the desperate hand wanking, until I told him he could dress me up as long as he didn't make me look ridiculous. His response was to buy me an American-style cheerleader's uniform. He got it by mail order, and for all I know it may have been for a real team, because it was certainly good quality. The top was sleeveless and quite tight, so that it clung to my breasts and let my nipples show through, and in blue

45

with a white trim. There was a heavy pleated skirt, white and blue, just long enough to cover my bum when I was standing still but guaranteed to show off my knickers if I bent over too far or jumped about. The knickers were blue and quite big, tight too, and there were blue socks with a white trim as well, and blue-and-white pom-poms.

It did make me feel sexy, and he loved it, even without heavy make-up, which was a first. When it arrived he came straight over to ask me to put it on, and I obliged. I thought his eyes were going to pop out of his head while I was getting dressed, and he'd got his cock out before I'd even managed to tie the blue ribbon in my hair for the pony-tail he wanted. There were pictures on the back of the packet of some moves the girls could do, and I tried a few out in front of him. Not many, because it was too much for him. I got put over the bed, my knickers pulled down and his cock slid up from behind, always his favourite way, and all this with my parents downstairs in the lounge and no lock on the door.

After that I was always a cheerleader for sex. He was obsessed with it and would spend ages on the bed wanking while I performed in front of him, doing all the moves we could find and more, especially the ones designed to show off my knickers. Bending to touch my toes was an obvious favourite, but he liked handstands a lot, and jumping so that my skirt would rise up over my bum. He liked me dishevelled too, with my knickers down under my skirt and my top pulled up to show my tits, but always in uniform.

Another favourite of his was to make me suck him off so that he could see in the mirror on my wardrobe. He'd sit on the bed, slobbed out with his back to the wall and his cock and balls sticking out of his jeans while I knelt between his legs to suck him.

He'd make me start fully dressed, usually, and he liked to put me through a little routine. First I had to turn my cheerleader skirt up to show my knickers, then it was back to sucking for a while, until he decided it was time for me to get my tits out. I'd lean back and pull up my top, showing off for him and playing with my tits until my nipples were hard, sometimes folding them around his erection and letting him titty fuck me for a while before taking him back in my mouth. He liked me to keep him in my mouth while I exposed myself behind, and to do it really slowly, pulling the big blue knickers tight over my cheeks and up between before taking them down, and he always insisted I leave them around my thighs.

Before that I never really used to come with him, but he liked to watch me play with myself while I sucked him, because of course he could see my bum and pussy in the mirror. It was always easy to get off that way, at first mainly because I had his cock in my mouth and could concentrate on my clit, but the more we did it the more I came to associate being in my cheerleader outfit with orgasm. I never got as bad as him, but ever since then there's been a connection in my head between showing off in uniform and sex, which was what allowed me to cope with working at Oh-La-La.

It was good, don't get me wrong, but I was never completely happy with him because it was really obvious that what he wanted was a cute cheerleader, or a Pierrot, or a girl made up to look like a golliwog, or whatever, but not me for my own sake. He was just too obsessive, and it got to the point where if I wasn't in my outfit he just couldn't be bothered, so in the end I dumped him.

Unfortunately it was too late, because even though my next man was a real caveman type and seemed to be more or less permanently hard for me I could never just come from friction alone and thinking about what we were doing. I had to fantasise, and it was nearly always about being put in some sexy little uniform and made to show myself off, so before long I was back in my blue-and-white cheerleader's outfit and over the bed with my knickers down and the new man up me from behind. Not that he minded, but I think from now on sex will never really feel right for me unless I'm somebody's doll.

Three

As I went to fetch another bottle I was wondering if it would be a good idea to have Kiara in her diminutive maid's outfit on a permanent basis. Her attitude seemed to me an odd mixture of resentment and excitement, but that's girls for you, and the thought of having her beautiful golden-skinned bottom peeping out from beneath the little black skirt was highly appealing.

By the time I got back Paul was holding forth on one of his favourite topics, his time in the army.

'Being in uniform makes all the difference in the world, and it's not just 'cause an army uniform looks smart, 'cause they don't, not all of them. Dress uniform, sure, but not battledress or fatigues, but when it comes to the girls it don't make much difference. It's the sense of danger, I reckon.'

'Not so much danger,' Angelique put in, 'more authority. I like a man with authority, and a good uniform says it all. You're wrong about the type not mattering as well. For me, it's the smarter the better, and the higher the rank the better.'

'You're right about rank,' Paul agreed. 'The night I made sergeant ...'

'Sergeant's good,' Angelique put in. 'Senior enough, but just a little bit rough.'

'Are you calling me rough?' Paul answered, obviously joking, but stretching out the fingers of his huge hands as he spoke.

Angelique gave an excited little squeal, but Kiara cut her off.

'Tell us about the night you made sergeant, Paul.'

That was only one time. I found out that a uniform does it for the girls right from the start. I was pretty crap as a teenager, you see, too shy, and broke too. Whoever I fancied, she always seemed to prefer some flash git with a load of patter and a car. I don't suppose I looked much either, at six four and skinny as a bean.

All that changed just about as soon as I'd joined up. I did my basic training at Pirbright, 'cause I was Royal Artillery, which soon beefed me up a bit, and the uniform is dead smart. The No. 1 dress uniform, anyway, which is dark blue, only of course you wouldn't normally wear that, not just out on the town. We used to go into Farnborough and Aldershot, mainly, sometimes up to London, and we always got plenty of attention from the girls. The blokes didn't like it, though – reckoned we were taking what was theirs, I suppose.

I lost my virginity on a night out like that. We were in Woking, we were, just going past the hospital on the way to the station, when this group of girls starts joking with us. Tanya, one was called, and it was like I didn't know what hit me. One minute she's joking around. The next she's taken my hand, and before I know it we're on our own in this big park. I only half knew what I was doing, but she did, and how. Tiny little thing, she was, with a narrow face, very pretty, but sort of sharp, with freckles and black hair done up in bunches. Innocent, she looked. Believe me, she was anything but.

Before we were even in the bushes her hands were all over me, stroking down the front of my buttons and stuff, like she couldn't get enough of me. She got dirty quick too. As soon as we were out of sight she had my dick out and in her mouth. But when I tried to get my trousers down to give her a bit more she wouldn't let me. She wanted me in uniform, you see, with just my dick out so we could do the business. That didn't stop her stripping off, though. I could see her, just about, and she didn't have enough hands for what she wanted to do, touching me all over and trying to get her knickers off and her tits out all at the same time.

I was stiff in no time, believe me, and what with the way she was sucking and her pretty face stuck on my cock and the way she was playing with her titties, I thought I was going to waste it in her mouth. She stopped just in time, pushed me down on the ground and climbed on top. I'd always imagined the moment my cock would go in a girl's cunt, how tight it would be and everything, and whether I'd have trouble finding the hole, but, with her, she just pops it in and starts riding me like she's demented. Rubbing herself on my dress trousers, she was, which made a right mess, and bouncing up and down, and all the time squeezing her tits in her hands. She got herself off like that, in maybe a minute, then she climbs off and lets me do my business in her mouth, and swallows too. That's the way to go, that was.

She wasn't the only one, either, over the years. I was never much for chatting girls up and that, but you don't have to be, not when you've got a uniform to do the talking for you, and, anyway, I always reckon that if a girl wants you she'll let you know, and, if she don't, she won't, simple as that. It don't always need to be smart either, not all the time.

51

I remember doing exercises on Dartmoor. There's a line of red flags and red-and-white striped posts and, when the flags are up, the army are supposed to stay inside the line and the civvies are supposed to stay outside it. 'Course, it don't always work that way, and if I had a quid for every time I've had to tell some silly sod to clear off unless he wants his head blown off I'd have ... enough for a decent drink, even in here.

Of course, when the silly sod's a nice-looking girl it's a bit different, but you've still got to do the right thing. She was just watching us, this girl, but from right up on top of the rocks by the flag, which wasn't really sensible. I was a bombardier by then, so it was me who got to go over and have a word with her. A fine sight I must have looked to her, with my battledress covered in mud and sheepshit, 'cause you can't keep away from it up there, and running sweat and all.

I knew straight off what she wanted, 'cause she wasn't exactly subtle about it, asking to feel my muscles and all. You wouldn't have thought it, not to look at her. About thirty, she must have been, with a la-di-da accent and a Burberry coat, but from the look in her eye I could see she was as bad as any of them. I took her down the other side of the rocks, I did, where the lads couldn't see, and I had her right there. She was well up for it, tits out and skirt up in no time, and I don't know what she'd done with her knickers, 'cause she didn't have any when we got down to it.

She wanted it all different ways, she did, with her on her back and me on top, kneeling down with her arse in the air, lying down sideways with one leg held up so I could watch it go in and out, and it was her who said that! She had beautiful skin, I remember, very pale and smooth as cream, but by the time I'd done with her she was filthy, mud all over her tits and in her hair, sheepshit all up the back of her expensive coat and on her bum where she'd sat in some while she sucked her own cream off my cock, the dirty bitch. She had me do it in her face too, honest, that was how she wanted it, right in her open mouth and all up one cheek, in her eye too. Loved it, she did, and I tell you straight, if I hadn't been a soldier and a bit dirty, she'd never have gone for it. I know, 'cause she told me after.

The posh ones are often the worst, you know, underneath. There was this major, the Piranha we used to call her. All she was was OC Personnel for the camp at Winchester, but the way she acted you'd have thought she was a field marshal, and the way she dressed too. Her uniform was always just right, tailor-made it was, and designed to show off her figure. She was tall, very slim and always just so, with seams in the back of her stockings and her hair tight up under her cap.

She lived in married quarters, with this little bloke, a civilian, and it was a rumour that sometimes she'd take some nice-looking boy from the ranks home with her and have the old man watch while she got a stiff one from the lad. My mate Steve claimed he'd had her, but I reckon he was full of shit, 'cause he made out she'd had her hubby watch the whole performance, naked and tied up, with her knickers stuffed in his mouth. Even they were khaki, so Steve said.

I'd like to have seen that, her with her smart skirt up and no knickers, perfect little arse in the air while Steve humped her from behind. Wouldn't have minded doing it myself either, only not with her old man watching and jerking on his willy. Enough to put anybody off, that. I don't know how a bloke can do

53

that, anyway, watch another guy fuck his missis, but it takes all sorts.

I was going to tell you about the day I got made up to sergeant. We went out for a few drinks afterwards, me and some of the other lads, in town, only this was Osnabruck, so half the British Army were there anyway. We were having a drink and a laugh, and my mates were telling anyone who'd listen how I was going to be sergeant and trying to cadge free drinks, and more. There were these two girls from Legal, and I suppose you lot would have got off on them, 'cause they were togged out in their dress uniforms, green jackets and skirts and that, only one of them had so much up front she was having trouble keeping it all in.

The lads started to tease them, saying they had to buy a round or get their tits out for us, and we're in this little alcove at the back of the pub, so, after a bit, out come their tits. You should have seen them. The smaller one, Miriam, she had a decent pair, about as big as a couple of good-sized oranges, say, and she opened right up, nice and slow. I watched every moment, as she opened the buttons of her jacket one by one, with her titties swelling out a little bit more every time, then the same with her blouse. You know the type, No. 2 dress, in army green, and they're never that generous, so any girl who's a bit heavy up top looks like they're trying to get out for some fresh air. Miriam's did, even with her jacket buttoned up tight, but with it open her whole blouse was just bursting with tit, and every button that come undone we could see a little bit more, the slit first, then her bra, with her titties sitting there like two pigs in a blanket.

We had to tease her a bit to get her to take her bra off, but she done it, reaching around her back to do the catch, then pulling it off down one sleeve, and when she takes her arm away, there they are, all round and bare. I was fit to bust, I can tell you, but the show wasn't over, not by a long way. The bigger girl, Helen, she'd said she wouldn't, and she'd watched Miriam doing her little strip like she couldn't believe her mate would have the nerve. So she's still buttoned up tight in her uniform while Miriam's holding them up for inspection, only now Helen's not getting any attention, and if there's one thing I've learnt about girls it's that they like the attention. So all of a sudden Helen gives this little cough, and I remember what she says like it was yesterday.

'Those aren't tits. These are tits.'

She's already got the top two buttons of her uniform jacket undone, but that's all. Then she starts on her blouse, not slow like her mate, but casual like, and she pulls it open as soon as she can, and she lifts those great big titties up out of her bra and sits them on her chest. She was huge, and, if Miriam's looked like they were trying to get out, Helen's look like they're about to explode, and 'cause of the way she's got them sticking out of her half-open uniform she's showing enough cleavage to park a bike, never mind your cock.

That's what I wanted to do, like any bloke would, have her hold them around my prick and give her a good titty fucking. They were game and all, giggling and showing off, even letting us touch them, but we couldn't do it there, not in the middle of a pub. When some bloke passed our alcove they both put them away, sharpish, and we thought the show was over, but oh, no. 'Course, after getting an eyeful of titty, all the boys wanted more, and, like I said, I've never been a great one for chatting up, so I didn't reckon on being one of the lucky ones.

Only I hadn't reckoned with those sergeant's stripes, had I? For the rest of the time in the pub both of them were giving me more and more attention and pretty well ignoring the others, and when we left they took an arm each. Didn't I feel good, walking down the road with those two on my arms, feeling their tits press to me, and the others as jealous as fuck.

I knew they were up for it, but the problem was, where? I couldn't take 'em back to barracks, any more than they could take me back, or I'd have lost the stripes I'd just got. So they took me down an alley round the back of this factory, and we did the business right there. Fuck me, but that was good. We found these steps, and they had me out of my trousers before we'd properly settled down, pulling on the old pud like they couldn't get enough. Just like Tanya, they were, the both of them. Didn't want me stripped, just wanted the important bits sticking out and the rest of my uniform just the way it was.

Personally, I like a bit more flesh, and I got them to take their titties back out, the way Helen had done, with the top of their jackets and blouses open and all the meat sticking out the top with a good deep slit between. I had 'em suck me, Miriam doing my balls while Helen took my prick in her mouth, then I titty fucked them, one at a time. Miriam was nice, folding 'em around my cock and jiggling them about, but she wasn't big enough to make a proper slide. Helen was, easy, so big only the tip of my prick stuck out between 'em, and, boy, did that feel good, hot and soft, and her still with her cap on her head.

I came like that. I couldn't stop myself, right up her titty slit and all over both of them, with Miriam giggling like crazy to see her friend get sploodged. She helped tidy up too, with some tissues she'd had in her bag, and that's another sight I won't forget in a hurry, two busty little army tarts, one wiping spunk off the other's titties. Not that they were lezzie or anything, I don't think, just good enough friends to help do the necessary.

And that was just the start of it. They hadn't had theirs, d'you see, and they weren't letting me get away before they had. Some of the late bars were still open, and we went drinking until I was ready again. That didn't take too long, not with those two cuddling up and pressing their tits against me, and all the time me remembering how they looked with their uniform tops open. We were on beer with schnapps chasers, which is quite some mixture, let me tell you, and by the time we came out of the third bar I was ready for anything, which was just as fucking well.

Angelique says she likes a man in uniform 'cause it gives him authority, and I can buy that. A lot of girls are like that, and when they are they usually want it a bit rough, or to get their bums slapped before you put it to them, that sort of thing. Helen and Miriam weren't like that. They liked my sergeant's stripes OK, and they were happy to be titty fucked, only not because it made me in charge of them or nothing. What they wanted was raw sex.

The bar was in the Frankenstrasse, and there's this huge railway siding, with a lot of waste ground alongside. That's where they took me and, when I say they took me, I mean it. Like before, they had my prick out of my trousers in double time, taking turns sucking and being greedy about who got her mouthful, until I put Miriam back on my balls. I played 'em a little trick too, pretending I was having trouble getting hard by thinking about kit inspection and stuff, then said I'd be better if I could watch 'em play with each other's titties. They weren't too sure, but Miriam already had hers out, with her jacket and blouse right open this time, and it wasn't long before they were at it, with Helen teasing Miriam's titties and Miriam trying to get Helen's out so she wasn't the only one showing 'em off.

That was a sight. Both of them with their uniform jackets and blouses wide open and their bras pulled up, titties on parade and feeling each other up while they took turns sucking my cock and balls. I could have spunked, easy, all over 'em, but they wanted theirs and, when they saw I was getting too randy, they told me they wanted fucking, and to get a condom on. That was all right by me, and I told 'em to get down side by side and I'd take turns with 'em from behind. They went for that all right, next to each other, with their titties swinging down while I turned up their uniform skirts and took down their knickers.

I fucked Miriam first, then Helen, riding on top of 'em with a tit in each hand, only I'd no sooner got my pace up in one than the other wanted me back. I tried to frig Miriam's cunt while I fucked Helen, but she wasn't having it, and before I knew what was going on Helen had wriggled out from under me and Miriam was pushing me down on the ground. I was too pissed and too horny to stop 'em, and I got Miriam's bum in my face while Helen climbed on my prick.

She had a big round arse, that Miriam, and I could hardly breathe, let alone lick like she wanted, what with Helen bouncing up and down on my prick and rubbing herself on me like she was demented. They took turns and all, and, if I'd thought Miriam had a big bum, she was nothing to Helen. I tell you, I was being smothered, and she was rubbing it right in my face to make me lick her arsehole as well as her cunt. I did it an' all, I was that horny, and she got off like that, same time as Miriam came on my cock.

I wasn't there yet, 'cause of having come before and what with the condom on and all, but they was nice about it, real ladylike. Helen stayed on my face, only not so hard, so I could enjoy her bum and cunt while Miriam tossed me off. Good, that was, like they were taking care of me, which reminds me of a nurse I knew when I lived in Pompey. She was like that, always considerate. Keeping me 'despunked', she used to call it.

That was just after I'd left the army. I had a bit of money put aside and figured on taking some time off before I started to look around for a job. A mate of mine said I could use this flat he had in return for doing a bit of work on it, and after a couple of weeks I met Barbara. Got chatting to her at the funfair on the front, I did.

'Course, I didn't have to get up, but she did, and she had this little routine every morning. I used to sleep through her alarm, no problem, and she'd wake me up with a cup of tea. Already dressed, she'd be, in her pale-blue uniform with a big white belt and a little hat. We'd talk while I had my tea and, of course, it being morning, I'd get hard. Sometimes she'd just get on with it, but she often kicked off with this little line.

'Right,' she'd say, 'let's get you despunked.'

Then she'd turn down my covers, just far enough, take out my cock and balls and toss me off, real matter of fact. She was good at it too, squeezing my balls and tickling my arsehole with one hand while she jerked me with the other, but she always did it the same way, like it was a necessary little job, just that and nothing more. She could be hot as Hell at other times, doing different positions and all sorts, but when she was in her uniform she was always really cool about it, and just wanked me off, cleaned up with a tissue, gave me a peck on the cheek and off to work she'd go. Maybe she reckoned it would keep me faithful if I was tossed off every morning, I don't know.

Or maybe it was just 'cause she liked to look after people, and so if I had an erection she dealt with it. She did it a few other times too, if I was horny and she wasn't. I remember meeting her from work for a drink at the Blue Anchor and trying to tease her into going back to the flat for a quickie. She didn't fancy it, but after a bit she gives me her usual line about getting despunked, takes me in the Ladies and tosses me off, just like that. It was the middle of the afternoon, of course, and nobody much about, but still . . .

Four

Paul trailed off, looking slightly embarrassed for his confessions, although he'd been open enough while he'd been going. Kitten shrugged.

'I've wanked men off like that, sometimes,' she said. 'It's no big deal, just a small favour. Anyway, I like cock, so, if a man asks, why not?'

'What, any man?' Kiara asked.

'Not any man,' Kitten answered her. 'Not if they're rude, or pushy, or whatnot, but for a boyfriend, sure, and if somebody's nice, and obviously needs it badly.'

She gave the same eloquent shrug she had before and John spoke up.

'Like a sympathy fuck, only a hand job?'

'Yeah, I suppose so,' Kitten agreed.

'They ought to offer it as a service on planes.' Angelique laughed, and put on her formal air-hostess voice as she went on. 'Coffee, tea, a drink, or would you like me to wank you off, sir?'

'You'd spend the whole flight doing it,' I pointed out. 'And what about the female passengers?'

Angelique giggled and made a gesture with one hand, as if cupping another woman's sex and using the longest finger to rub between the lips. Vanity made a little purring noise in her throat and was going to speak, but Paul got in first.

'Were you really an air hostess, then?'

'No,' Angelique admitted, 'and I never wanted to be. I know it's supposed to be a glamorous, sexy job, but I don't reckon the reality would be up to much. I'd only get sacked for shagging in the toilets or sucking the pilot off anyway, like I got the sack from my tour-guide job. I prefer stripping and burlesque.'

'You look the part,' Paul continued.

'Thanks,' she said. 'It's a real uniform, one I nicked from a flatmate after we had a bust-up over how much rent she was paying. She thought she should be let off some of it because she was away so much of the time. She was with some French company, doing short-haul flights all over Europe, but I don't suppose she even got fucked in her uniform by her boyfriend, never mind a passenger, silly bitch. It looks better on me anyway, and I've put it to better use. Like you, Violet, I love people to think I'm the real thing, but the only time I've worn a uniform as part of an ordinary job was when I was a tour guide, and that didn't last long.'

'Tell us,' Violet demanded.

I'd better give you some background first. I was always what my parents used to called highly sexed, and as a teenager I could never understand why people were so disapproving about it. I liked my body and the sensations I could give myself, and the way boys reacted to me. It was all just fun to me, and I was a terrible tease, flirting with anyone who'd react and tormenting the ones who wouldn't. I was at quite a staid school, and I was forever getting told off for wearing my skirts too short or leaving too many buttons undone on my blouse, but the more they told me off the more I resented it.

I like to shock anyway, just to see the expression on some prude's face because they caught a glimpse of my knickers, because when it comes down to it they're just being stupid, aren't they? I mean, we're all naked underneath our clothes, aren't we? It's ridiculous to be ashamed of our own bodies. A lot of people are, though, and maybe I'm an evil little bitch, but I love to get a rise out of the prudes, and to treat the ones who appreciate it. OK, so I don't give sympathy wanks, but I get the idea.

Basically I'm an exhibitionist, and I like it to be rude, but I don't like it to be too blatant. The thing about flashing yourself is you want it to be a shock, so, if you come on stage as Pippa the Stripper and go all the way, it's no big deal. The audience have come to see a striptease, so it's what they expect, and it's worse if you start off in some tarty outfit. That's why I prefer burlesque, because the audience don't know how far you're going to go, so I can work up my comedy routine until they think that's the full deal, and then they get to see my bum.

It's even better when they're not expecting anything sexual at all, because then you really get a reaction, and not just shock. I've found that men get far more turned on by an unexpected glimpse of something naughty than a full-on display when they knew that's what was on offer, and it's even better if you can make it look like an accident. That's one reason I like my air-hostess uniform. A lot of people expect you to be a bit aloof or proper, so it's even more fun showing off. But I was going to tell you about my experience as a tour guide.

First the uniform, as you're a bunch of perverts. Like when you're an air hostess or even just working in a smart office, the uniform was designed to display a woman's figure while still being demure. It was bottle-green with a black trim, and consisted of a knee-length skirt and a jacket, tailored to show off my hips and waist. There was a little green hat to go with it, and we were told to wear black tights and smart black shoes with an inch of heel. That was all written down in my contract, and I always used to imagine an inspector making me pull up my skirt to check that I was wearing tights and not stockings. If he had, he'd have got a surprise, as while I wore a slip with it for comfort I often used to go commando. I love the sensation of being smartly dressed in a respectable situation and having no knickers on. It's deliciously naughty, and the thought of giving an accidental peep of pussy or deliberately parading my bare bottom is such a turn-on.

We specialised in coach trips for wealthy tourists, Americans mainly, who wanted to see the sights of old England. Stratford was popular, and Windsor Castle or anything to do with the royal family. Also Tintagel, which we used to say was Camelot, and that meant a weekend trip with a day spent showing the tourists around. That was the worst route, because you would not believe how demanding elderly American tourists can be, like expecting a particular brand of bottled water from some spring in the Rockies while standing on top of a fucking cliff in Cornwall.

I don't suppose I'd have looked twice at Mick, the driver, in normal circumstances, but when you're thrown together like that, just him and me to cope with forty Yanks, it tends to form a bond. He was well into me anyway, and in a way I like, obviously impressed but assuming he'd get rejected. It's the uniform, you see, because it makes me look so stuck up, even when he was wearing the same . . . not the skirt, obviously, but you know what I mean.

I used to tease him, like bending down to help a passenger so that my bum rounded out my uniform skirt behind when I knew it was pretty well right in his face. That turned me on and helped pass the time too. If he'd got dirty with me I think I'd have backed off, and if he hadn't reacted at all I'd have got fed up with it eventually, but he used to let it get to him, and to me that is just asking for trouble. I'd catch him looking at the swell of my bum under my skirt or the way my tits pushed out the front of my uniform jacket, and he just looked so hungry.

That was the first Tintagel trip, and I had a woman driver on the second, but for the third I was back with Mick again. When I climbed onto the coach to tell him he had me as guide he looked like a sick puppy, and I'd already decided to torment him as we loaded up the group of geriatric New Englanders we were taking down to the West Country.

With a trip like that the first hour or so is always chaos. Mick had to get out of London, which kept his mind on the driving, while I had to cope with everything from some git who expected us to detour back to his hotel near the Tower just so he could pick up his spare glasses to a mad old bat who kept asking questions about Princess Diana. It was only once we'd got out on the motorway that things began to settle down, and by the time we were past Reading I was bored.

The time before, I'd made out everything I did was a complete accident, so Mick had no idea I even realised the effect I had on him. That was OK, but it left him with a cop-out, because he could always tell himself it was all in his mind. This time I decided to torment him properly, so I came forward to speak to him, asked a couple of innocent questions about our progress, and then whispered in his ear.

'I've got no knickers on under my uniform.'

I'd waited until we were on a nice straight stretch of road before I said it, which was just as well, because he jumped like somebody had given him a kick up the arse. He threw me a great look too, surprise and excitement and doubt all at once, as if he couldn't quite believe what he was hearing. I gave him a smile and walked back down the bus, letting his imagination work.

He'd think it was a come-on, I was sure, but only after he'd thought it through for a bit, because I'd always been so aloof with him before. So I waited five minutes while I explained to a couple from Rhode Island that the woods we were going through were not Sherwood Forest, then went back to the front and squatted down next to Mick again. This time he gave me a dirty grin, which I wiped off his face with a single line.

'But you don't get to see.'

I was struggling not to laugh as I walked away again, imagining what he'd be thinking, wondering how I could wind him up even more and whether I dared. He was anything but aggressive and very careful of his job, so I decided it was safe and quickly went back, again whispering into his ear.

'Or maybe you do. Just think, Mick, no knickers.'

This time he reacted openly, throwing me a pleading look and speaking.

'Don't say things you don't mean.'

'It's true,' I told him.

'Yeah, right,' he answered, and gave a little scoffing laugh. 'I know your sort. You're just trying to wind me up.'

He was right, but I hate being caught out like that, and, anyway, I was telling the truth, because I'd decided to spice up the trip a bit by deliberately going commando all the time, knowing it would keep me on a high the whole weekend, which was the only way I could get through it. I knew he was playing me at my own game, but as always my reaction was to go right back at him.

Our coaches were huge, with a built-in loo and a big luggage compartment, so that the passengers were sitting high up and there was a little flight of steps leading up from the doors by the driver. That meant the only person who could see the little flat area down by the doors was Mick. Just about everyone had settled down, and quite a few looked as if they'd be asleep before long, while for once nobody seemed to be paying much attention to me. I couldn't stop myself.

'Oh yes?' I told him. 'Watch this.'

I was going to flash him, and it was a great feeling, because while the passengers couldn't see me the doors were glass and the windscreen came down so low that just about my whole body was visible to any passing motorist who happened to glance my way. The motorway was quite busy too, and as I walked down the steps I was thinking of the show I'd be making and how public it was. My knickers would have been soaking if I'd had any on, and I was seriously nervous but determined to go through with it, no matter what.

Mick kept glancing at me, so I gave him a wink and began to lift the front of my uniform skirt, very slowly, meaning to give him just the briefest flash of pussy, which I reckoned would be enough to prove I meant it and keep him on edge for the entire weekend. I nearly did it too, but then I realised I could be meaner still, and stopped. I saw him swallow, and he was going to speak again, but stopped as I turned around.

'Uh, uh, that's too special for you,' I told him. 'Like they say, the tradesmen's entrance is around the back.'

That hit home, and I'm sure he muttered 'bitch' under his breath, which for me is just asking for trouble. I was still looking at him, eye to eye, as I started to lift my uniform skirt again, only this time high enough to give him a brief peep of my bare bum cheeks before I covered myself up again. That should have been enough, and I saw him swallow, but he came back at me.

'Yeah, right. You're got a thong on, that's all.'

'No, I haven't,' I answered him, in a hiss because some of the passengers were a bit close.

'Yeah, right,' he repeated.

I decided on a new tactic, making him feel he's filthy, always a good one with men who aren't that secure about themselves. Coming back up the steps, I whispered into his ear again.

'You just want to perve over my pussy, don't you, you dirty little bastard?'

'Me dirty?' he answered. 'You're the one pretending you've got no knickers on under your uniform.'

I could've slapped the little sod, but he was getting to me, while the kick as I flashed my bum cheeks had made me want more. He was challenging me, too, and I needed to win.

'OK,' I told him. 'I'll show you. I'll show you something you can never, ever have.'

'You haven't got the guts,' he answered.

It was a blatant come-on, too blatant really, but I was feeling horny and determined to leave him seriously frustrated.

'Oh, haven't I?' I said, and went back down the steps.

He took a glance at me as I once more started to pull up my uniform skirt and, again, just in time to get a peep of my pussy. You know I shave, because you've all seen, so he got everything, not just a bit of hair. I don't think he realised I would go through with it, and maybe he really thought I was lying about having no knickers, because he swore under his breath and had to quickly grip the wheel to keep control of the coach.

That scared me a bit and I left off. Anyway, I had him, because as I climbed back up the stairs I could see the shape made by his cock where it was sticking down one leg of his trousers. He was fully erect, a long green bulge in his uniform, which must have been seriously uncomfortable and embarrassing too. I gave him a smile and a wink and got called a bitch again, then left him like he was and went to ask if anybody wanted tea.

What I'd done was enough to keep me happy for the rest of the morning, just thinking about that hard bulge down the leg of his uniform trousers and how he knew that I was bare under my skirt. If the loo hadn't been so busy I'd have gone and played with myself, but only after telling him what I was doing, another thought that helped keep me on a high until we reached Glastonbury.

I had to do my tour-guide bit, while Mick stayed in the coach, so there was no chance of any more mischief then, but I'd got myself in such a state that I couldn't calm down. Just to feel my bottom cheeks and pussy mound move against the inside of my slip was driving me crazy, and this image of how I looked had fixed in my mind, so smart and respectable in my green and black uniform with my hair up and the little cap on my head, but with no knickers underneath.

A hundred and one fantasies were going through my head. Climbing the Tor so people could see up my skirt. Flashing the tourists right then and there.

Pretending I'd left something in the coach and going down on Mick in his little compartment, with hundreds of people about who could see his upper body but would never know he had his tour guide sucking his cock. Even taking some of the better-looking male tourists in among the bushes and asking if they'd like to have me as an optional extra.

None of it was practical, and I ended up back on the coach hornier than ever. I could see Mick was hoping for more too, from the look he gave me as I jumped onboard after checking the last of the tourists in, and I stayed down in the space by the door when we set off, meaning to give him another peep, only to get called up to the passengers because some dozy old git couldn't get his seatbelt on properly.

By the time I'd sorted all the passengers out we were back on the motorway and I'd cooled down a bit – enough to want to tease Mick rather than suck his cock, anyway. I went down into the space by the door again and sat myself down on the little pull-down seat there, but with my skirt a little up and my knees apart, so that anyone kneeling in the well would have been able to see my pussy.

Mick knew, and kept glancing at me, but there was no way he could crane around far enough to see. That was good, and I was sure his cock would be getting hard again, so I gave him a wink and inched my skirt up a little more, showing some thigh. He knew I was teasing and tried not to look, but he couldn't keep his eyes off me, glancing down again and again. When I got called up again, sure enough, Mick's cock had begun to snake down his trouser leg, maybe not as hard as before, but getting on that way.

I gave him a smile to make sure he knew I'd seen, then called him a dirty little boy when I came back.

He called me a bitch again, and told me to stop it, so I knew I was getting to him. A lot of the passengers were asleep again, and those who weren't were pretty somnolent, as most of them had put away as much for lunch as I'd eat in a week. I wanted to be bad, really bad, to do something so rude I'd shock myself and not just Mick. There was another thing too, which you'll probably think is weird, but I knew that if I didn't get myself off I'd end up with his cock in me that night, and I didn't actually want that.

So I frigged off right there on the pull-down seat, in front of Mick, so he knew what I was doing but couldn't see anything more than I wanted to show. Some lads in a minibus that passed us did, though, just as I got my uniform skirt up mid-thigh and opened my legs. After that there was no going back. They'd seen my pussy, a brief but unmistakable flash. The way I was, Mick could see my thighs up to just above my stocking tops, so he had a little bare flesh to perv over, but nothing that really mattered, while of course he didn't dare do more than glance at me occasionally.

He could see what I was up to, though, no mistake, with my knees apart and my hand up my skirt. I was absolutely soaking, so wet I was scared it would soak through my skirt and let everybody see just what a bad girl I was, but that wasn't going to stop me. If anything it made me worse, and as I teased myself I was thinking of how I'd flashed my bum and pussy to Mick and how hard his cock had been, how the lads in the minibus had seen me bare and that they'd probably be wanking over me that very night, but mostly I was thinking of how good it would be to just take my soiled skirt off and go about my duties with my bottom showing bare under the tails of my uniform jacket and my pussy peeping out at the front.

That was the image I needed, myself in uniform only not just with no knickers but with no skirt either, pussy and bum bare to the world as I worked. I was wishing I had the guts to really do it, and imagining all the shocked faces and disapproving remarks, the way the men would be trying to get a better view while pretending to be outraged ... but, best of all, how Mick would finally lose patience with me for being such a tease, take his big fat cock out of his uniform trousers, rip my blouse open, bend me over in the aisle of the coach and stuff it up me for a good, hard, public fucking.

I came over that, picturing myself in the aisle of that coach, gripping desperately onto the rails with my bare tits swinging in the ruins of my smart little blouse and uniform jacket, my skirt and knickers already off and my bum stuck out as Mick thrust up me from behind – only right at the peak of my orgasm it got even worse. I remembered how I'd teased him over showing my pussy, and what I'd said to put him down, that the tradesmen's entrance was around the back. In my mind I thought of him repeating my own words back to me in front of the entire coachload of American tourists as he forced his cock up my bumhole.

That was some orgasm, and I know it's dirty, but I didn't actually do it, not with Mick. I like to think of the dirtiest possible thing when I come too, because I get the best orgasm that way. Anyway, that would have been that, only that idiot Mick had turned on the coach security camera so he could film me having my frig. Even that wouldn't have been so bad, although I'd have killed him if I found out, but the prat didn't remove it immediately after we got back, so the inspector was treated to a full-on video of me rubbing my pussy off. They even made me watch a bit of it when I was pulled into the office, and, as you can imagine, that was the end of my career as a tour guide.

Not that I was actually sacked for masturbating on the job, not in so many words. The letter I got just went on about distracting the driver, not being sufficiently attentive to the needs of our customers and 'general misconduct'. Bunch of miserable bastards, the lot of them.

After that it all got a bit fucked up for a while, but I had promised myself never to take on a job where I'd have to do as I was told by some stuck-up creep, and I've kept to that. Not that it was easy, without much in the way of qualifications or references, but the more I thought about it the more I figured I'd make a good stripper. I'm not hung up about my body and I can handle men, so why not?

Like I explained, it's not really a turn-on for me, not when it's what everyone expects, and after a while you get used to it anyway. In fact, I spent so much time walking around stark naked in front of a load of men that I began to worry I'd lose the thrill of showing myself off completely. I was always getting pressured to get my tits done, dye my hair, get tats and piercings and lots of other shit too, so, while nobody could actually order me to do anything, there were still too many people who thought they could.

That's why I put together my burlesque act, although I still do a bit of pole dancing and stuff when I need the money. I was stripping full-time when I nicked the air-hostess uniform, but I only used it a couple of times because, like I said, having the audience know it was coming off spoilt the fun. Misbehaving in it while pretending to be the real thing is better by far.

Just being dressed like that is a kick, especially if men approach me because they fancy my image as an air hostess. I suppose it's a bit like the way Kiara likes to be seen as a doll, but there's definitely a hit from having a man fixated on the way I look rather than on me as such, and isn't that always the way anyway, at least a bit? Whatever. To a lot of men air hostess spells sexual availability and sexual sophistication at the same time, and that's a great mixture.

For a start they're always out to impress, which means fancy wine bars and champagne, because for some reason they always think that's what you're used to. I really play up to the image too, passing on all the stuff I've heard from my ex-flatmate, who was forever dropping into the conversation the names of the places she's been and the celebrities she's met. Once or twice I've come unstuck, with men who've actually been around a bit, but most of the time they just lap it all up.

Believe me, they can be desperately eager to please, but those are the ones who generally just end up buying me drinks all night. Mick the driver may have been a prat, but at least he knew how to tease back, and he almost got what he wanted. If men are too easy I don't usually go through with it, and for all my behaviour I'm quite fussy when it comes down to it. It was like that the first time, with a guy who met me in a bar where I'd dropped in for a quick drink on my way to the club where I was stripping. He was drooling over me, or rather he was drooling over my uniform, and particularly the way my tits filled out the blouse.

He really thought he was it, snapping his fingers at the barman to order a bottle of champagne and explaining to me which the best houses were and why you should only ever drink a few well-known names.

I soaked it all up, and as we drank I pretended to get horny for him, letting my leg touch his, then undoing the second button of my blouse right in front of him. He nearly popped his own cork at that, and by the time we were getting near the bottom of the bottle I'd undone another button to give him a peep of the edge of the lace bra I was wearing. By then the bulge in his trousers was about three times the size it had been, and he wasn't talking to me at all, but to the opening of my uniform jacket where he could see down my cleavage.

When he suggested going back to his flat it was obvious he was sure I'd accept, and I did, telling him I just needed to powder my nose first. That was the phrase my flatmate always used, and it's just what they expect of an air hostess. I left him looking like the cat that's got the cream, headed for the loos and then nipped out of a side door. I know that's bad of me, but he was such a wanker.

The first time I actually went for it was because the guy was just so fucking cheeky. I was on my way to a stag do, where they'd asked for an air-hostess strip, and because it was hot and I wanted to try and get into the mood I decided to walk there fully dressed. A lot of men were looking, as usual, including this one black kid who can't have been more than nineteen. He was on a bike, and when he saw me he cycled on to where I was going to have to cross a footbridge over a main road, quite obviously intending to look up my skirt and not even trying to pretend otherwise.

I wasn't sure if I wanted to give him a treat or wind him up, but there was no way I could avoid reacting to him – that's just not me. Unfortunately if I didn't cross the bridge I was going to have to go far out of my way, so it was impossible to prevent him looking.

I was tempted to confront him, but all the little bastard had to do was deny it, or just laugh at me, and he looked the sort. So I decided to play up to my image and crossed the bridge with my nose in the air and my legs as close together as possible. He watched, and wolf-whistled me, although he can't have seen much, then followed.

That was actually scary, because he seemed to have no idea at all about what was acceptable and what wasn't, but I was in full view of a couple of hundred motorists on the bridge, so when he caught up with me I stopped, intending to give him a piece of my mind.

'Do you mind not staring at me?' I demanded.

'You wish, lady,' he answered, and laughed.

I'm not used to men like that, and the idea that I should want his attention rather than the other way around was so outrageous I didn't know what to say, especially as he'd just been trying to look up my skirt. What he said next was worse.

'Buy me a drink. Maybe I'll give you one.'

He can't have thought I'd accept, no way, so he was obviously just trying to get a rise out of me, and he'd succeeded. I just had to turn the tables on him.

'Why don't you buy me a drink?' I suggested.

'Got no money,' he answered.

That wasn't the answer I'd been expecting, and it took me back a bit, but now turning him down because he was broke was going to make me look like a pro, which I was a bit sensitive about, what with working as a stripper and everything. I was still trying to work out my response when he came out with his next bit of cheek.

'How about we go back to my place? No one's in.'

God knows I've been propositioned often enough, but for sheer cheek he really took the prize. I came close to telling him to fuck off, but there was still that feeling I might not be safe, and I didn't want to antagonise him. For the second time I failed to find a worthwhile answer before he spoke.

'You're posh, you know that? I like posh girls.'

It was supposed to be a compliment.

'I bet you do,' I answered him.

'And posh girls, they like boys like me, yeah? So very special, you think you are, in your fancy gear, but what you want is a piece of black cock. That's right, ain't it?'

Now he really had me stumped. How are you supposed to respond when a man says something like that? He was so wrong too, because it had never occurred to me to think about him in that way. But there was obviously no point in denying it, as he didn't seem to be able to see outside his own head. My silence only made it worse.

'Yeah, I've got your number, ain't I?' he went on, grinning. 'I've never had a trolley dolly, but I'm going to now, and you can stay in your gear while I fuck you.'

It was hard to take in his sheer arrogance, and I'd gone pink with embarrassment at the thought of being had in my uniform by a man like him – well, a boy really. Up until then I hadn't realised just how much he was getting off on the fact that I was in uniform, either. What mattered to him was that I was an air hostess, or so he thought, and he wanted sex with an air hostess. That was what mattered to me too, to be fucked as an air hostess, and even while I stood there stammering out a disgusted denial I'd decided to go for it. Only I still wanted to salvage some pride, so I told myself I'd have some fun with him, and then afterwards when he was full of himself I'd confess that I was a stripper, which would really burst his bubble.

'You've got me,' I admitted with a shrug. 'Let's go.'

I knew I was taking a risk, and being an utter slut, but sometimes you just have to go with it. He even had the nerve to get on his bike, leaving me to walk a little behind, but his house wasn't far at all, in among an estate of newly built red-brick boxes a little along the main road. Inside it was neat and tidy. He obviously lived with his parents and he'd admitted as much, but it was his room that really got to me. His walls were covered in posters for Arsenal and the bands he liked, all very boyish, and there I was, a grown-up air hostess seduced into taking a fucking.

Normally I'm terrible, flirting and teasing until the man's fit to burst and then maybe putting out or maybe not. I like to keep a man unsure, but now I'd agreed he could fuck me and I no longer felt in control. The way he looked at me got to me too, grinning and full of himself, like he was completely sure that there was nothing I wanted more in the whole wide world than to be made to pleasure him.

And didn't he just make me. I think he must have been watching too many pornos, because he'd barely closed the door before he'd got his cock out and put me down on it, grinning at me while I sucked him erect and telling me how sexy I looked in my uniform. He knew just what he wanted too, as if he'd got the whole thing scripted in advance, like a sort of ritual for how to make the best use of a sexually compliant air hostess.

First I was made to open my blouse and push my tits up while I was still sucking him. He used my cleavage for a cock slide, and I'll swear his eyes were as much on my open uniform jacket as my breasts. Next he had me take my knickers off and wrap them around his cock while I wanked him, and all the time

78

he was talking at me as if I was the one getting the treat, going on about his big black cock and how I wanted it up my 'white trolley-dolly pussy', his actual words.

Then came the fucking. First it was bent over his bed, staring at the 2005 Arsenal team while he pulled my skirt up and slid it in from behind, with my tits swinging and him slapping against my bum as he fucked me. He was a dirty bastard too, telling me how good I looked with my skirt pulled up and my bum bare, how he could see his cock going in and out of my pussy and how my bumhole was showing to him. I didn't care any more. I just wanted his cock, up my pussy and in my mouth too, at the same time if that had been possible.

Boy, did I get it. Once he'd had his fill of looking at my bum he rolled me over and penetrated me so that he was standing over me as I lay on the bed with my legs rolled up. He couldn't keep his eyes still, flicking them between the junction of his cock and my pussy, where it showed under the edge of my uniform skirt, and my open jacket and blouse – really drinking me in, a dishevelled air hostess, tits bare and penetrated on his bed. I just gave in to it, playing with my tits and rubbing myself while he fucked me, and I'd have happily come like that, only he wasn't finished.

He made us change around, with him lying on the bed and me on top, so he could hold my uniform open and watch my tits bounce as I rode him. Then it was the same position only backwards, with me holding my own skirt up to show my bum and his thumbs on my cheeks so he could see between. I knew what he was getting off on too, because he kept telling me how I looked with my uniform disarranged and his cock sliding in and out of my cunt hole.

Something about the way he said that really got to me, and I had to come. I stayed on him, moving gently up and down while I rubbed at my clit and picturing how he saw me, an air hostess still in my smart blue uniform but with my tits and bum bare and his big black cock stuck in my pussy, my cunt hole as he'd called it. He'd seen what I was doing too, and was laughing at me and calling me his bitch as I came, which added a last filthy touch to my orgasm.

He'd come too, right up me, but fortunately I'm on the pill so it didn't matter. Afterwards he was so pleased with himself, thinking he'd fucked an air hostess, and in the end I didn't have the heart to tell him otherwise. It's funny, though, because I can just imagine him boasting about his conquest, and all the time I'm ready to strip off for a few quid and there's nothing I like better than showing off my body, in uniform or out of it. I never did get to that stag party.

I never saw him again, either, and do you know? I don't even know his name. Maybe it's just as well, because everything between us was based on fantasy, but he was good. He gave me more confidence too, not that I needed much, and taught me to see how so much of sexual pleasure is what's going on in your head and not reality at all. After all, there is no difference between a real air hostess and me dressed as an air hostess, not unless there's a plane involved, and if my ex-flatmate's anything to go by I bet I'm ten times better than the real thing.

Jerry Sheldon didn't see it that way, but then he was a real obsessive. He's also about the only man to have worn me down through sheer persistence. You must have all met men like that, who keep at it until you either give in or get a restraining order, and Jerry Sheldon was mine.

After my encounter with the black kid, I took to wearing my uniform more and more, in fact just about all the time if it wasn't at the dry cleaners. I was making quite decent money, so I could give more time to indulging my love of exhibitionism and what was becoming an increasingly powerful fetish. I even considered trying to get a job with an airline, but it's not at all easy to get into, especially for a stripper, and, besides, I was worried that the reality might spoil the fantasy. I'm not a complete nutcase, by the way. I've only ever pretended to be an air hostess for show, or sex, and of course to wind up men.

Jerry started off like that. He lived quite close to me, and we often passed in the street. He'd really stare, so much so I swear I could feel his eyes on me even with my back turned. I'm used to that, and I like it, but this was something else, and I knew it was to do with my uniform, because when he saw me dressed any other way he'd always look disappointed.

That sort of thing tempts me to tease, and I began to make a point of pretending to adjust a shoe or dropping something when he was watching, so that I could bend to show off a bit more leg and let him admire the shape of my bum under my skirt. I was in the same tube as him one time too, sitting down while he was standing, and I deliberately undid two buttons so that he could see down the front of my uniform blouse, as well as about a dozen other men.

I'd guessed he was plucking up the courage to make a move on me, and I'd already decided to turn him down. He wasn't my type, really, not enough guts, or so I thought, and when he came up to me in the street with a bunch of those cheap roses you get from blokes at road junctions I just stuck my nose in the air and walked right past him. That didn't put him off, and it didn't stop me teasing him either. In fact, the worse he got, the worse I got.

There was an old church near by, with a big flight of steps and two benches at the top on either side of the doors. I knew full well that if any woman in a skirt sat there she needed to keep her knees together or she'd have half the perverts in the district looking up her skirt, so if the weather was warm I often used to have my lunch there, deliberately leaving my knees a little open so that they could get a peep at my knickers, or even my bare pussy if I'd gone commando that day.

Jerry wasn't a typical Peeping Tom, but when he saw me there and realised he could see up my skirt it was more than he could resist. It got him in a right state too, because he knew he could only walk back and forth so many times before I started to get suspicious, but he couldn't keep away. I just ignored him, as if he didn't exist, but having turned him down gave me a special thrill and I'd soon let my legs slip a bit further apart while I ate my sandwich and pretended to daydream, blissfully unaware of what I was showing.

I was in white knickers, which are always best for giving a panty show because they leave no doubt in the voyeur's mind about what he's seen, but after the fourth or fifth time Jerry had walked past I was wishing I'd gone commando, so that he could go home with a stiff cock and an image of my bare pussy in his head, knowing he wasn't going to get it.

Eventually his embarrassment got the better of him and he went off, or so I thought, only to have him come back a few minutes later with another bunch of roses and a huge box of chocolates. This time he gave me the full spiel, about how much he adored me and how it would mean so much to him if I even agreed to let him buy me a coffee, and more of the same. I had my answer ready long before he'd finished.

'It's not me you want to go out with, is it? It's my uniform.'

I didn't think a man could actually go the colour of a beetroot, but Jerry did, and I knew my comment had hit home. He started stammering denials, of course, but he was obviously lying, and he knew I knew. I waited until he'd worked himself into a complete state, then gave him a single word.

'Pervert.'

For a moment I thought he was going to burst into tears and I felt a complete bitch, but he managed to keep himself under control and made some lame remark about proving his love to me and not giving up. At least, I thought it was a lame remark, but he really meant it, as I found out. I'm my own worst enemy sometimes, because I should have had the sense to stop teasing him, but oh, no, not me. I was back on the same bench the next day, only without any knickers on and my legs just a little bit apart so that anybody who chose to look would get a peep of newly shaved pussy.

He must have been watching from somewhere, because he turned up after maybe ten minutes, only instead of trying to catch a sneaky peek up my skirt he came and knelt in front of me on the steps so that I had to quickly close my legs or risk giving him a close-up, which was more than I'd bargained for. He had the chocolates and flowers, the same flowers actually, which were a bit wilted and slightly spoilt the effect. I was a bit taken aback and tried to be sensible about it, telling him that he wasn't my type, which was the truth. He just nodded and went away, so I thought that was that.

It wasn't. I didn't see him for about a week, but when I did he followed me and asked me out again, this time without even bothering to back himself up with a gift. I turned him down again, not quite as politely as before, and he went away, but he was back the next day, having found out where I lived. After that he began to become a real pain, always hanging around me and trying to talk to me, which in a way I suppose is justice for me being such a flirt, but it was a pain. Even telling him I had a boyfriend didn't make any difference, presumably because he was watching me and knew I was lying.

The only odd thing is that he never figured out I wasn't a real air hostess, presumably because he so badly wanted me to be one, or maybe he was just thick. Anyway, in the end I decided that the best thing was to go on a couple of dates with him and hope he'd lose interest. The first time he took me to an Italian restaurant, and he was so desperate to impress and to agree with me about everything that it bored me rigid. He seemed to enjoy it, though, and to think he was winning, because he didn't push it afterwards, not even trying for a goodnight kiss, but simply running one finger down the sleeve of my uniform jacket as if he was touching some sacred object.

I'd agreed to another date, because I wanted him to feel he'd had a relationship of sorts and that I wasn't worth his while, before ending it as tactfully as I could. The second date was much like the first, but on the third he invited me up to his flat for coffee. I accepted, meaning to spin him a line about saving myself for the right man, in the hope that it would put him off, but to my horror he agreed with me.

As you can imagine, I was kicking myself after that, but it seemed sensible that if he liked me pure and virginal he might be put off if he thought I was a slut. So on the fourth date I let myself get a little drunk and started telling him about my sex life, or, at least, my supposed sex life, which consisted of all the normal bullshit you associate with air-hostess fantasies; joining the mile-high club in the loo of a Jumbo with a guy I basically described as James Bond, sucking off a randomly selected celeb in first class and getting gang-banged by a group of drunken Taiwanese businessmen.

To my annoyance he just soaked it all up, only interrupting to make sure I'd kept my full uniform on for the entire performance. I challenge anyone to describe being spit-roasted by four men without getting at least a little horny, especially after an entire bottle of Valpolicella, so by the end of the meal I'd decided to take him home and let him fuck me, just to get it over with.

I didn't want him to do me in my uniform though, because that would have spoiled my own fantasy, so when we got back to his flat I gave him a nice slow striptease and then told him to join me in bed once he'd had a shower. So in I went, and waited, and waited, and do you know what the little bastard did? Do you?

He laid out my air-hostess uniform on his living-room floor and wanked over it, that's what. He was still doing it when I came back out, and I caught him just in time to see it come out, all over my skirt and jacket, with his hand jerking up and down on his little weedy cock so fast it was a blur and his face set in an expression I can only describe as demented.

The moment he'd finished and realised I was watching he started stammering apologies, but he was basically telling me that my uniform was so lovely he couldn't help himself, and this with me standing in the doorway, stark naked! I could have killed the little runt, but I made the mistake of demanding that he take my uniform to the dry cleaners, which of course meant I had to see him again.

He did what he was told, and when he brought my uniform back he was begging for another chance. I really couldn't face it, so I did what I should have done in the first place and told him I wasn't a real air hostess at all. He wouldn't believe me at first, so I showed him some pics of me stripping and a really dirty one some guy took at a stag night where I'm in full uniform only with my tits out and rubbing shaving foam into the groom-to-be's cock and balls so I could shave him.

I hadn't expected Jerry to be happy about it, but I didn't expect him to burst into tears either, or to call me a cheating, lying whore and a lot worse, which is just weird when you think about it, because he was well into me being rogered senseless by Taiwanese businessmen, who I'd told him had paid me to do it, but he couldn't handle me being a stripper and abusing his precious fantasy uniform at all. Stupid bastard.

Talking of bastards, I have to tell you about John, the guy who's first ever words to me were 'stuck-up bitch'. Charming, I'm sure you'll agree, and he had a huge chip on his shoulder about the middle class. To hear him talk, you'd have thought that anyone with their own house and a professional job was some sort of drooling bogeyman bent on doing down the working man, whom he thought of as saintly and persecuted.

He was all in favour of strippers, of course, but as a persecuted minority group rather than because he liked to watch girls take their clothes off. But air hostesses, oh dear. To him air hostesses symbolised everything that was wrong with the world, so when I accidentally jogged his elbow in a pub I got called a stuck-up bitch. I just thought it was funny, at first, once I'd got over my surprise and a bit of annoyance, but there was actually something quite horny about the situation. He was a big guy, with really muscular arms and a lot of tats, not the sort who'd take any nonsense if I flirted with him.

Still, I'd have let it go if a friend hadn't told me about his attitude, and that got me thinking. I could just imagine him going to bed with me thinking I was an air hostess. He'd really take it out on me, and, so long as he did it with his cock and not his fists, that was a serious turn-on. I wasn't too sure about it, though, and made some careful enquiries, but he seemed to be quite safe – safe enough for my horniness to overcome my qualms, anyway.

I had to play it right, so that he'd go for it but wouldn't turn soppy on me, so I decided to drop a hint via our mutual friends that I liked it rough and thought he was about as rough as they come. The idea was to make him feel a little bit insulted and horny at the same time, so he'd take me up on it and really put me through my paces. Just knowing I'd sent out the message was a serious thrill, and scary too.

Really I should have gone a bit slower, but I couldn't waste any time because there was a fair chance he'd find out the truth before he got to fuck me. So the next time he and I were in the same pub – just after I'd done a burlesque strip and been dancing naked for about two hundred guys at a working man's club, incidentally – I pretended to get drunk and started coming on to him in a really haughty way, as if I was trying to pick him up as a bit of rough for my casual amusement.

He went for it, and as he walked me back towards the bedsit where he lived I was absolutely melting inside. His arm was around me, with one hand on my bum, kneading my flesh through the skirt of my uniform so that everyone we passed saw what he was doing. He really wanted to show off, and if he'd tried to have me across the bonnet of a car or just on my back in the middle of the street I'd have had trouble resisting. I was soaking too, which was just as well, because he'd no sooner got me indoors than he pushed me down on the bed. When he spoke it was like a bear growling.

'So you like it rough, do you?'

I'd meant to try and be bossy with him, in the hope that he'd overcome me and get off on using me by making me suck his balls, but my resistance had gone right out of me. I could only nod, thinking of all the things he might make me do and how he wouldn't take any nonsense about it anyway. He laughed at me and unzipped himself, pulling out one of the biggest cocks I've ever seen: not so much long as enormously fat, enough to really stretch my pussy.

He didn't even bother to make me suck it, unfortunately, but simply grabbed my legs and rolled me up, holding both my ankles in one hand as he jerked my uniform skirt high. I'd half thought he might strip me, but he wanted to fuck an air hostess, and all he did was pull my knickers up off my legs. He spread me out so he could see everything, grinning at what I was showing and how he imagined I'd be feeling about being put on display like that. He called me a dirty stuck-up bitch when he saw how wet I was, then climbed on top and just stuck it up with one push.

It was like being fucked by a bear – not that I have been, but still. He just took hold of me and jammed himself deep, with his whole weight on my body as he started to thrust in and out so hard and so fast I immediately lost my breath. I'd never been fucked so hard, and it was like he'd completely taken over my body, but I thought it would be over quickly, a short, vicious fucking ending with him coming inside me and leaving me used on the bed in my soiled air-hostess uniform with his come dripping out of my pussy.

I couldn't have been more wrong. He kept thrusting himself into me until I was faint with reaction, then stopped, pulled out and started to use me. First he climbed further up the bed, his thighs spread across my body, growling an order as he thrust his cock at my mouth.

'See how your cunt tastes, bitch. Suck your cream off me.'

I sucked. Not that I had much option, because he'd taken me by my hair, and the moment I opened my mouth I got his cock jammed halfway down my throat. My legs were still up and I knew just how I'd look, with my uniform skirt rucked up and my pussy spread and open, him on top of me as I struggled to suck up my own juice – as if I was being raped, only I wasn't, because my only problem was that I couldn't get my hands to my pussy to bring myself off while he did me in my mouth.

Again I thought he was going to come, either down my throat or in my face, and I was imagining how I'd look in my dishevelled uniform with my pussy agape and a mouthful of spunk or my face plastered with it while I brought myself off in front of him over what he'd done. Only he still wasn't finished.

'Now your tits,' he growled, and before I could protest he'd ripped my blouse wide open and pushed them up out of my bra to make himself a cock slide in my cleavage.

There was nothing I could do but take it, and I still couldn't get my hands to my pussy. He was really rough about it, crushing my tits around his cock and pumping like mad, with his knob popping up and down between them. This time I was sure he wouldn't be able to hold himself, and I opened my mouth to have it filled with spunk, being openly dirty for him. I got called a dirty bitch for my trouble, and had my face slapped but I was so high that that just made me worse.

He seemed to be determined to use me in every possible way while he had me, not so much for the physical pleasure of it but to deliberately degrade me, because I was an air hostess. Just then, that was exactly what I wanted, which was why I didn't even put up a fight when he rolled me over onto my face and told me he was going to put it up my bum.

I was still underneath him, completely trapped, and he was manipulating my body as if I was a ragdoll. As soon as I was bum up he jerked my uniform skirt up around my waist and pulled my jacket down to trap my arms, then began to rub himself in my slit. That felt so scary, pinned down helpless with a big man rubbing his erection between my cheeks and knowing he was going to put it up my bumhole, but I wouldn't have tried to stop him even if I'd had the choice.

He did at least lube me up, sort of, sticking his cock back up my pussy to get some juice between my cheeks and sticking one finger up to open me. I'd pushed my bum up to take him more easily, which got me called a dirty bitch again and earned me a few hard slaps across my cheeks while he fingered my hole, but it was what he said next that really got to me.

'Now it's going up you, you stuck up little middle-class bitch, a working man's cock, right up your perfect little arsehole.'

With that he put his cock down between my cheeks and began to push. I felt myself start to open up, which is just weird, like being fucked in the pussy only as if you're on the loo at the same time, and so dirty. I had to come while he did it to me, I just had to, but I couldn't get my hand under my tummy because as he jammed himself up me he'd let his weight settle on my back.

I was swearing at him and telling him to let me get my hand to my cunt – my exact words, and most unladylike perhaps – but he didn't seem to notice, calling me a middle-class bitch over and over again as he forced the whole length of his cock in up my poor bumhole. I said he was big, and especially thick, and by the time he'd got it all in I felt like I'd had a marrow stuffed up my bum. That got worse when he started to bugger me, ramming himself in and out so hard he was knocking the breath out of my body with every thrust, and I was writhing like crazy underneath him, furious because I couldn't get a hand to myself and finish off while he was doing it.

He didn't care, though. He just wanted to use me. Maybe he even got off on denying me my orgasm: that, or he wanted to make me save it for the final degradation, which was yet to come. When he stopped I thought he'd spunked up my bum, but he hadn't. He growled at me as he pulled himself slowly out of my aching hole.

'I'm going to teach you a lesson you'll never forget, bitch. Next time you go past some hard-working bloke with your nose in the air, remember how I fucked your arse, and remember this.'

As he spoke he rolled me back over, one-handed. He'd lifted his body to do it, and my hand went straight to my cunt, rubbing like crazy. I'd guessed what he was going to do to me, and I just had to come. He had me by my hair again, his cock pointed right at my mouth as he grunted out an order.

'Suck it, bitch.'

I held off for maybe two seconds, not because I didn't want to do it, but because I wanted to get the image of myself clear in my head: a pretty, middle-class air hostess being utterly used in a grubby bedsit, my uniform a mess, my tits out, my pussy and bumhole well fucked, and about to be made to suck the cock which had just been up my bottom. I did it, too. I sucked his dirty cock and swallowed his spunk while I went through the most blinding orgasm of my entire life. So now you know why I like people to think I'm an air hostess.

Five

She stopped speaking with a sudden, embarrassed grin, leaving absolute silence, each of us alone with our thoughts. I closed my eyes and tried to think about something other than what the man had done to her, in the vain hope that my erection would go down at least a little. It was Violet who finally spoke.

'You're worse than me!'

'Maybe,' Angelique admitted, 'but we each have to get our fix in our own way.'

'That's true enough,' Violet agreed. 'What about you, Richard? You got this whole thing together, so I suppose you're well into uniforms?'

'Yes, of course,' I admitted. 'Otherwise why bother? But my own appreciation of uniforms is different, more vicarious, and also catholic. I'll dress up myself, but only really to fit in with the theme, as my pleasure comes from seeing a woman in uniform, and so long as her body image suits the uniform she's chosen I don't much mind what it is. Take tonight, for example. All of you look delightful, and if asked to judge I'd find it impossible to choose between you.'

'You must have some preference,' Vanity objected.

'No,' I insisted. 'Let me explain, and also how I think it all works. My philosophy of uniform fetishism, if you like.'

* * *

To me, a uniform serves as a way for somebody to express their sexuality. Most of you seem to think it makes a lot of difference whether a uniform is real or not, but I don't see it that way. Yes, the real uniforms and what's associated with them have created sexual associations, and, as Angelique has explained in the case of the air hostess, they're often false. That doesn't really matter. What does matter is the image and our ability to enjoy it, exploit it if you prefer. Yes, you need real policewomen, schoolgirls, soldiers or whatever to create the image which becomes sexualised, but they don't have to be into it themselves. In fact, if they are, as Violet discovered, it can cause problems.

Much better, surely, to take your pleasure in playing a role and in having other people play theirs. That way all you need is a good imagination and a willing partner with appropriate tastes. You can play any role, according to the mood of the moment, and with none of the risks you'd have to run if the roles you've adopted were real. I can be a headmaster and spank a naughty schoolgirl, or a burglar who's caught and made to submit to a sadistic police-woman. Obviously some of you would argue that only the real thing is worthwhile and role play can never be more than a pale imitation, but to me that just shows a lack of imagination.

My ideal would be to have a partner whom I can dress up like a doll and, however she's dressed, that's who she becomes. I freely admit that I'm being impossibly selfish, and that any real woman will have her own wants and needs, but I can dream, can't I? So imagine I've got my doll, naked, and I'm going to dress her up. I might make her a policewoman, a nurse or maybe something in the army, but let's say she's a schoolgirl.

I'll call her Ginny, and say she's eighteen. She's a little above average height and naturally slender. The next thing is to dress her up, so let's start at her feet. Her shoes are black, made of shiny patent leather with a neat little strap-and-buckle fastening, just an inch or so of heel marked by splashes of mud. She is in long white socks, encasing slim, coltish legs to just a few inches above her knees, above which smooth, rounded thighs rise bare to the hem of her skirt. When she is older her long legs will give her elegance and poise, but for now she is just a little knock-kneed, clumsy, vulnerable.

Her skirt is tartan, pleated and loose. It is also scandalously short, on purpose, floating around her legs as she walks to provide constant, teasing glimpses of bare thigh. She is fully aware of the effect her body has on men, and finds this both amusing and exciting, while she loves to court official disapproval. By cutting off six inches and making a new hem she has ensured that with the slightest puff of wind she risks showing her knickers, while should she bend to adjust the buckles on her shoes she will be providing a rear view calculated to give a young man a hard-on and an old man a heart attack.

Should you be lucky enough to see her knickers, and it's always an option, you will find that they are plain white cotton and a little too tight, showing the heart-shaped bulge of her newly ripe sex in front, hugging the sweetly turned cheeks of her small but perfectly feminine bottom behind. They come up quite high too, keeping her flesh perfectly encased. Not that she needs support. She is gloriously firm.

Her skirt is worn low on her hips, and if it's a hot day she likes to show off, maybe with her blouse knotted under her breasts, leaving her midriff bare. Smooth, golden skin curves gently to the groove of her back, the line of her waist and the gentle swell of her belly, dipping in to form a tiny, tight tummy button which hints at the other, equally tight but far more intimate orifices.

The material of her blouse is a light cotton, and ever so slightly see-through. She has no bra on, because she doesn't need one, at least not for support. Her breasts are young, firm, high and somewhat turned up. Some people, her mother included, might argue that she needs a bra for decency, because her nipples peep out through her blouse, erect and angled slightly upwards in a manner that is highly sexual and provocative to the point of impudence.

She has a tie on, decorated with stripes in the red and black of her school colours, but it is undone. So are the top three buttons of her blouse, affording the chance of a glimpse of nipple to anyone in a position to look down it. Her sleeves are rolled up, showing bare arms, while her neck is long and elegant, her chin held high, full of confidence and pride.

Her hair is straight and a dark, glossy brown, tied back with a big red ribbon in a bow to form a long pony-tail that bobs and swishes as she walks. She has a delicate, oval face, a small mouth but full lips, unpainted and slightly parted to hint at what is hidden between her thighs. Her nose is small and a little turned up in exactly the same way as her nipples. There is a splash of freckles across the tops of her cheeks, beneath sparkling brown eyes that hold a world of mischief and erotic possibilities.

There we have her, my idealised fantasy schoolgirl, and while it would be nice to have a partner who actually looks like her I don't mind a few minor differences. What's important is that to have her dressed like that and behaving like that makes her a schoolgirl for me, and of course the more her dress and behaviour suit her, the better the fantasy, and the sex, will be. So what to do with Ginny?

If it's just in your imagination it can be anything you like; the possibilities are endless. Even if she's flesh and blood there's no shortage of choice. At the most basic it would be nice to have her suck me off, a sweet little schoolgirl down on her knees with her blouse undone to show off those darling titties and her panties down at the back, her pussy wet and ready for me once she's got my cock to straining erection in her mouth.

Or how about something a little fruitier? Maybe it would be nice to spank her? Why not? Schoolgirls are made for spanking, after all. Yes, I should put her across my knee for a good old-fashioned spanking, her skirt turned up, her big white panties pulled down and her neat little cheeks smacked red while she kicks and wriggles and squeals in an agony of stinging skin and embarrassment at the exposure of her pussy and bottom hole.

Then again it might be necessary to be a bit more severe with her. She is eighteen, after all. How about delivering six of the best across her pert little rump with a school cane – after making her take down her knickers and touch her toes, naturally? That would make her squeal. Yes, that's the way to treat a schoolgirl, knickers down for spanking and the cane. Not a real schoolgirl, of course – they'd lock me up and throw away the key – but she would look as good, react as well, and of course I can fuck her afterwards.

Of course it's better still if there are two schoolgirls to play with, and I always find that women are far more willing to let themselves go when it's just role play and there's no emotional involvement. So Ginny can have a friend. Let's call her Sophie, a plump little thing with big tits that always seem to be about to burst free of her blouse, and a bottom so chubby that her skirt doesn't cover it completely and she has the underside of her tight white knickers more or less permanently on show.

Now I can put the two of them on a bed to enjoy a slow, sensual *soixante-neuf*, while I watch, or perhaps spank and cane them side by side, or make one of them a prefect and have her do it to the other. If they swing I can probably squeeze a double blow-job out of them, maybe after they've been punished so that their bare red bums are stuck out behind while they suck me.

There are endless opportunities for exhibitionism too. I could take them down to the local park to play tennis or basketball, with both of them giving enticing flashes of those tight white panties every time they move and half the male population of the district trying not to stare. Or I could even take them dogging, and allow a few dirty old men to watch as we kiss and cuddle, with their tits out of their blouses, before I put them over the back seat, turn up their school skirts and pop down their panties for a side-by-side fucking.

Just imagine: the men watching wouldn't know we were role playing. I'd be getting all the pleasure of having two pretty bottoms framed between tartan school skirts and lowered white panties, and the girls would be enjoying giving a show and being fucked. Meanwhile, the voyeurs would be sure to enjoy the show and, if they liked, they could think they were watching two real schoolgirls get it from behind in the back of a car.

Looking at it from your side, girls, perhaps you might want to imagine yourself as her, and do things you never could in normal life but might like to as a highly sexed and highly attractive schoolgirl. How would it feel to be Ginny while she has her well-endowed young boyfriend's cock in her hand, her mouth, her pussy? How would it feel to be her while she has the dirty old janitor's cock up her bum? How about when she gets that spanking for cutting her skirts short, or gets carried away with a school friend and ends up in a tangle of tongues and tits and slippery fingers pushed down the front of each other's panties? It's all possible, and at no risk whatsoever.

That said, in my ideal world I could go beyond the possible and treat her as if she really was a doll, subject to my every whim, and the world around us would have to be rather more flexible as well. After all, as Violet's made only too clear, it can be risky to have to operate in the real world. That's what I'd really like, a girl to play with as if she were a doll and in whatever setting amused me. For instance, after I'd got bored with having Ginny as a schoolgirl I'd strip her down, stark naked, baby bare, with even the ribbon in her hair gone. She'd still be beautiful, and delightfully vulnerable, with an expression of shock on her face and her hands pressed to her pussy and tits in a largely futile effort to cover up what she's got, but she wouldn't be a schoolgirl any more, because she wouldn't look like one.

Let's imagine she's our doll. It's not really fair to leave her in the nude, so let's give the poor little thing some clothes. We did make her a bit of a slut, didn't we, with that tiny skirt and no bra? This time, let's take a different angle. Being eighteen, she's still at school, but she's a navy cadet and a senior one at that. Her shoes are equally smart but more sensible, in sturdy black leather with a big solid heel. The long white socks are gone, replaced by dark, hold-up stockings that reach well up under her skirt, which is knee-length and made of dark-blue wool, practical and designed to ensure that there is not the slightest risk of her giving an accidental display of stocking top or thigh, let alone her panties.

Her blouse is in heavy-duty cotton of a slightly paler blue, and done up properly, as is her navy tie. On top of this she has a jacket, cut to suit her figure but unmistakably nautical, with the crossed anchors and crown that show her rank on each sleeve. This time she has a bra on, oh, and knickers, obviously. Her hair is up, in a tight bun beneath her cap, while her air of flirtatious mischief had been replaced by a look of uncompromising severity.

Now who's going to put her on her knees for a BJ or spank her little bottom for her? You would? Fair enough, there's always room for an uncompromisingly Neanderthal attitude, Paul, and for unbending dominance, but in either case you are responding to her rather than to her uniform – unless, just possibly, you happen to be a ranking naval officer? No, I thought not.

Come on, her new look is far more appropriate for an assertive or even dominant role. She certainly wouldn't be just plain Ginny any more, but Petty Officer Virginia Milne, and she might well be the one demanding that you get on your knees and provide oral sex, or even applying a rope's end to your buttocks. Then again, depending on your personal tastes, it might be more fun to watch while a junior cadet gets put through her paces.

We can have Sophie back, also in the uniform of a naval cadet, but there are no insignia on her sleeves and she carries herself very differently, full of enthusiasm but a trifle nervous. Despite her best efforts, there is an untidiness about her ash-blonde bob, with several unruly wisps escaping from beneath her cap.

Her face is soft and pretty, with a full mouth and large blue eyes, which are currently filled with apprehension and no surprise.

She is standing to attention in the long spartan barrack room which the squad are occupying as part of their training, and she has made the serious mistake of being the last to get up for breakfast. Perhaps she did it on purpose, perhaps not, but both she and Virginia know that for the next half an hour there is little or no chance of them being disturbed. That is why Sophie has her uniform skirt rolled up to her waist and her chubby pink bottom pulled out of her panties so that her own hairbrush can be applied to her bare cheeks.

The smacks are hard, and they hurt. As you peer in through the window you can see the way the muscles of her bottom and thighs tense in anticipation of the brush strokes, and how her flesh quivers at each impact. You can hear her gasps and squeals too, and the cruel humour in Virginia's voice as she chides her victim. After a while Sophie is made to turn around, providing you with a different but equally exciting view. Her blouse is undone and her large firm breasts have been lifted out of her bra, sitting fat and naked on her chest to add to her humiliation, her nipples stiff in the cool air. You can see her pussy too, a plump pink mound lightly grown with golden-blonde hair and noticeably puffy sex lips with a deep slit between, from which a little juice has begun to trickle as she grows aroused despite herself.

A pretty view, don't you agree? Or perhaps you prefer Virginia to take her pleasure in inflicting humiliation but not pain? In that case poor Sophie still has her knickers up, but she will be earnestly wishing she can pull them down, because she has been made to drink two litres of water and she knows that at any moment she is going to wet herself.

You have a prime view of her cheeky bottom bulging in her tight white panties, or from the front, if you prefer, with the cotton taut over the lower part of her chubby little tummy and showing the outline of her sex. She is begging to be let off, but either she won't dare to cross Virginia or she'll want to do it in her knickers for all her protests, you won't know which. You'll be able to hear her clearly, and see her rising panic as the pressure in her bladder grows, until at last it becomes too much and she lets her pee come out, trickling down her legs and splashing on the floor beneath her, spreading in a wet stain up over her bottom cheeks and cunt.

We are being rather mean to poor Sophie, aren't we? Perhaps it would be better if Virginia was simply to seduce her? Imagine the two of them playing together in their smart blue uniforms, Virginia gradually teasing Sophie into opening her blouse, rolling up her skirt, lifting her bra, taking down her panties, leaving her dishevelled and ready for action.

They can be intimate, if you like, lovers trading nervous kisses, as full of defiance for those who would seek to deny them their feelings as they are of desire for each other. Their caresses will be tender, gentle, fingers stroking necks and backs and faces, timid at first but with growing urgency as their excitement rises and their inhibitions flee. Only gradually will they conquer their shyness, but soon enough they will be giggling as they compare their breasts, Virginia's high and firm, Sophie's round and heavy.

Soon both their uniforms will be in disarray, blouses open and bras up, navy-blue skirts rolled high and knickers pushed down as they clutch at each other's flesh, exploring, probing, fingers slipping in up moist excited holes, tongues pushed deep in each other's mouth. They'll be too wrapped up in each other to care about the risks any more, going down onto one of the beds, tangled together with their bottoms in each other's face, busily licking pussy.

Shall we let them get away with it? It would be kind, wouldn't it? At least let's let them come, with Sophie wriggling her bottom in Ginny's face as she gasps out her ecstasy, before returning the favour, to leave them cuddled together in a giggling, happy heap. That's when they get caught, not by another girl but by the teacher who's in charge of them, or a naval rating from HMS *Tresco*, where they're doing their training.

In reality, everything would now become extremely tedious and extremely unpleasant, with concern expressed and steps taken and a lot of little, beetle-like people scurrying around in an effort to destroy the girls' love for each other in the manner dictated by modern social theory. Expressions like 'inappropriate behaviour' and 'for their own good' would be used, leaving the beetle-like people solemn but smug and the girls devastated.

Fortunately, this is not reality. If the girls are caught by their teacher she can spank their naughty bottoms for them, which they will enjoy despite their tears. The rating, a man, is going to want something rather more. There will be a great many protests, made more for the sake of saving face than from any real objection, but the girls will end up kneeling together with their tits out of their uniform blouses as they lick and suck at his cock, right up to orgasm and a sticky faceful for each of them, by which time they'll have their hands down each other's panties.

Sassy schoolgirl or sadistic naval cadet, slut or lover, aggressor or victim, Ginny is a delight, a beautiful plaything, a doll. We can dress her as we please, strip her and dress her again, with her personality and behaviour dictated by the uniform we put her in, just like the toy she is, a grown-up, imaginary dolly created for the expression of our sexual fantasies.

Reality is not necessarily so very different. A uniform is normally functional, defining a person's appearance and therefore their role in society: how they will act and how others will respond to them. Neither action nor response is normally sexual, but it can be. Being in uniform can make you the object of desire to somebody who would otherwise be indifferent, which is the essence of fetishism. To put on a uniform can also allow you to express your sexuality, whether the uniform is real or adopted, and allow others to express their sexuality with you. It makes you into something different, and that something can be changed with a change of clothes, so that in effect you have made yourself a doll, to be played with for your own pleasure, or for the pleasure of others.

Ginny represents an ideal, and in the nature of ideals it can never be realised, but I would like to think I've at least come close. I'll tell you about Wendy the traffic warden, who was probably the closest I came. Like the military or police, I suppose some people may think of a traffic warden as a symbol of authority, but I bet they're the exception. To me, they're a symbol of being a bloody nuisance. Everything about the image begs for a good spanking. I mean, what red-blooded male wouldn't want to spank a pretty traffic warden, or a not so very pretty one for that matter?

Just imagine, turning up that smart black skirt, nice and slowly, so she can feel every moment of the anger and helplessness that she's inflicted on so many motorists. I'd really draw it out, and I'd explain to her what I could see as her thighs and bum came bare. I wouldn't take her knickers down straight away though. I'd start the spanking with them up, so she could think she'd got away without going bare-bottom, but once she was nice and rosy I'd stop and tell her. She'd start fighting again, but I'd keep a good firm grip on her and down they'd come, laying her bare.

Ideally it would be in front of a crowd, a big crowd composed of all the men and women she's given tickets to, and not one of them with the slightest sympathy for her. In fact, they'd clap and cheer as I got her bum bare, adding to her humiliation, and, of course, how could I resist playing to my audience? I'd pull her bottom cheeks apart to make sure they all got a good look at her anus, and maybe stick something up it, like her pen. I'd spread her pussy too, to let everyone see if she was still virgin, and all the while she'd be kicking and screaming her head off, but she still wouldn't get any sympathy, not even from the other women in the crowd.

Only once I'd brought her humiliation up so strong it couldn't get any worse would I spank her, hard, really hard, first with my hand and then with her own shoe. She'd absolutely howl, screaming and yelling, begging me to stop and in floods of tears, kicking and thrashing around so hard I might even have to ask for helpers from the crowd to hold her down. There'd be no shortage of volunteers, naturally, and I'd soon have her held firmly in place while I continued the spanking with her completely helpless. Perhaps I'd stuff her knickers in her mouth to shut her up, or maybe not. No, it would be better to enjoy her screams and hear her pleading for mercy.

I wouldn't stop until her bum was the colour of a ripe cherry. When I was finally done with her I'd strip her naked and leave her with her pen stuck up her bum and only her pad of tickets to cover her modesty, much to the amusement of the onlookers. And, if you think that sounds harsh, imagine the sort of person who will take a job the main purpose of which is to inflict misery on her fellow human beings. I mean, I wouldn't mind if they only gave tickets to people who were badly parked, but the way they do it now is sheer daylight robbery . . .

Anyway, never mind that. Where was I? Oh, yes, spanking a traffic warden. If you really did that you'd be in serious trouble, although it might almost be worth it, but in play you can still take a lot of your aggression out on your girlfriend's bum, although you do need to pick a girlfriend who's seriously into punishment. Wendy was like that. She liked to be spanked and it turned her on, but it was no good doing it as a sexual thing. It had to be a genuine punishment.

That's not actually all that easy. You can do the domestic discipline thing, and spank them for not tidying up properly or overspending on the credit card, but Wendy was naturally tidy and careful with money too. On the other hand I wanted her to be my doll and dress her up in uniform, so we reached what I still think was a clever compromise. She would get a job as a traffic warden, which would be easy because the council would employ chimpanzees if they could be taught to stick tickets on cars, and then I could punish her in her smart uniform, both of us knowing that she thoroughly deserved it.

Everything went smoothly at first, and the only difficulty was choosing which service had the smartest uniform. I was keen on the old-fashioned police version: you know, black with a yellow trim, which looks good and more importantly is the one I've been used to all my life. Wendy's blonde, and she felt the yellow clashed with her hair. She preferred the local council uniform, which was also a smart skirt suit, but dove-grey with a deep-red trim and hat band.

In the end I managed to talk her round and she had no difficulty at all in signing up. There were only two snags, the horrible yellow reflective jacket she was supposed to wear, which spoilt her image, and the fact that she was supposed to leave her uniform at work. That wasn't too hard to get round, though, because she was on a local beat and could easily nip in to get her spanking and be back out on the street in twenty minutes.

I remember the first time as if it was yesterday. She knew she was going to get it, which could be guaranteed to keep her wet and ready, and, having had trouble with two of her colleagues while trying to take a delivery in that morning, I was just in the mood for it. When she came in I had to do a double take to make sure it was her, in full uniform with her hair up under her hat. She looked adorable, so pretty and yet so ... so desperately in need of having her bottom smacked.

You all know the uniform, of course: sensible black shoes with a small heel, dark tights under a knee-length skirt which is part of a black figure-hugging uniform suit with a white blouse underneath, a tie and a cute little bowler hat with a black and yellow band around it. Just watching her take her reflective jacket off was enough to get my cock hard, and when she told me she'd already given out fifteen tickets that morning it left no doubt in my mind, or in hers, that she richly deserved what she was about to get.

I didn't waste any time, but whipped her smartly across my knee in the back office and set to work, skirt up, tights and knickers down and my hand applied to her naked bottom. She squealed delightfully, and it wasn't fake either, because I hadn't warmed her up at all but started in full force. I got her legs kicking too, which I love, and I must have given her a couple of hundred before I even paused for breath, by which time her entire bottom was glowing pink and she was in tears.

She loved to cry when she was spanked, but she could only ever do it if things were just right, so I knew our scheme was a success. I wasn't finished with her, though, not by a long way. Her knickers were around her ankles by then, so I took them right off and put them in my pocket, telling her she'd have to go bare under her uniform skirt for the rest of the day. She complained about that, because she had to change with the other girls and they'd all see, but that only made me more determined, so I told her to pretend she'd had an accident in her knickers and had to throw them away.

We did that three or four times before she gave up the job. Like I was saying before, reality is usually a poor substitute for fantasy, and she couldn't handle the abuse she got on the streets. The occasional bare-bottom public spanking from an aggrieved motorist would have been fine, just her thing in fact, but of course that's not what you get. However, she did manage to keep her uniform, by the simple trick of reporting sick in the middle of the day and not coming back. We had far more fun afterwards and, for the moralists among you, I would contend that just having been a traffic warden is reason enough for a lifetime of spankings.

Naturally most of our play was in the bedroom or the kitchen, where Wendy could be spanked and then fucked at leisure. There really is nothing quite so appealing as a woman in uniform with her bottom bare and red from punishment, although having her breasts exposed as well does add a certain something, and my favourite thing was to spank her and then take her from behind. I notice that a lot of you either prefer rear entry or for the woman to be on top, presumably because both positions allow you to enjoy being in uniform, while in missionary you can't really see what you're doing.

Wendy's favourite fantasy was to be done over the bonnet of a car, and not just spanked but fucked afterwards, and in front of witnesses. That struck me as too risky, because some idiot was sure not to appreciate the justice of the thing, and call the police. But she wanted it so badly I promised to do it, though somewhere private. My choice was a lay-by on what was once a main road but has since been bypassed, and in November to make doubly sure we weren't caught.

It did work, and we played out the whole scene, with Wendy pretending to ticket my car and me catching her, forcing her down over the bonnet, stripping her bum for a vigorous spanking, fucking her and leaving her there with come all over her red cheeks. She was so turned on that she stayed in position to masturbate, which had me wishing I could rise to the occasion a second time in quick succession.

Unfortunately that didn't satisfy her craving but only made it worse. She wanted the shame of being seen, and preferably by a large and approving audience. I did think of various ways it could be done, such as using a back alley next to a railway track so that people would see from the passing trains, but now that everybody has mobile phones it was too risky.

We tried again in a dogging car park, but that didn't really work either, because Wendy was always too much the realist and couldn't get off properly when she knew everyone was wondering what a traffic warden was doing out at one in the morning in a car park that didn't even have a pay and display machine. We did it anyway, but all we got was a queue of men hoping to take their turn with her over the bonnet of my car, which wasn't the idea at all. I made her hold her pose while some of them tossed themselves off in the bushes, which she found extremely humiliating, but it didn't answer her need.

By then she was far more into it than I was. For me, it was enough to have her in uniform and do it in the comfort and privacy of the bedroom, allowing my imagination to fill in the gaps, but for her that simply wasn't enough. At least one witness had to see and to think he was watching a real traffic warden being given a real punishment, but, as she would insist on being fucked after the spanking, that meant it would look like not just assault but assault and rape.

I didn't want to risk that, as you can imagine, but she kept pestering me until I finally agreed. It took me a lot of trouble to set up, so I was in no mood for any nonsense from her on the day. The place I'd chosen was a beach car park on the Norfolk coast, miles from anywhere and very exposed, so I could be sure it would be empty on a winter's morning. In summer it was quite busy, and you know how greedy councils are, so there was a pay and display system in operation from March to October.

Wendy knew the date, but nothing else, so I got her up early and made her dress up in her uniform, then drove out to the coast. She was disappointed when she realised how remote the place was, but changed her mind when she saw the three other cars parked there. Two were empty, but there was a young man in the third, staring blankly out to sea. He was a bit shocked to see a traffic warden, and immediately went to the machine, then returned to his car after finding out he was safe.

I'd parked by then, having dropped her off a few hundred yards down the narrow lane that leads to the beach, and I went down to the beach to watch the waves for a while. I'd planned it out like a military operation, calculating the time needed to spank her, fuck her and let her come before we retreated, but there were an awful lot of things that might have gone wrong, so I was feeling pretty nervous as I climbed the low cliff back up to the car park.

As arranged, she'd put a ticket on my car, and naturally I took issue with her. We started an argument, with the young man watching sidelong as I yelled at her and she explained to me that once a ticket had been issued she had no power to take it back, but that I had seven days to appeal in writing to the local authority – you know, the usual bullshit. It's odd, because my temper really did rise, and I wasn't gentle when I finally pretended to lose it and forced her down over the bonnet of the car.

It must have been pretty real for her too, because she fought like anything, screaming at me to get off and trying to scratch me, so that I had to twist her arm behind her back before I could get her skirt up. By then another man had turned up, with his dog, but he stopped at the edge of the car park, staring as I jerked Wendy's skirt up over her hips, with her fighting every inch of the way.

By that point I no longer cared about the subtleties of the situation. I was going to have her knickers down and spank her no matter what the consequences, but she seemed equally determined that it wasn't going to happen. She fought like a demon to stop those knickers coming down and her pussy getting an airing, clutching on to them with furious strength, and so hard that they'd pulled right up between her cheeks anyway, showing everything except those two last rude details.

In the end her knickers tore and I think it was her gasp of shock and humiliation as her bum came bare, and she realised that at long last she was showing it all in public, that really brought out the devil in me. She'd stopped fighting too, the instant her pussy came bare, and I was able to remove the remnants of her knickers and get her in position properly with her bum stuck well up and her legs a little apart to make sure the watching men got the best possible view as I spanked her, with nothing left to the imagination except the strength of her feelings, and it wasn't hard to guess those.

She did look beautiful too, with her little hat slightly askew but the upper part of her uniform otherwise immaculate, but her bottom stark naked and her pussy lips peeping out from between her thighs. I was already hard, and it was tempting to fuck her then and there, but I'd promised her a spanking and that was what she was going to get.

I laid in hard, smacking her across the fat of her cheeks and lecturing her as I did it. She burst into tears in no time, thick, broken sobs, with her face alternately looking shocked and pained or screwed up in what I swear was genuine misery and shame. I didn't let up, though, but kept on spanking until her whole bottom was aglow and my hand was almost as pink and sore as her flesh. By then all three drivers were there, keeping their distance but making very sure they didn't miss a single instant of the show.

Wendy may have forgotten she was to be fucked, or it may just have been an act, but her squeal of outrage when she saw me free my cock from my trousers was highly convincing. She wasn't going anywhere, though, because I had her arm twisted tight up into the small of her back. I had no trouble penetrating her either, because I was rock-hard and she was so wet I only had to push once and I was all the way in.

What a fuss she made as I fucked her! She was screaming obscenities and struggling in my grip, blubbering her eyes out and yet gasping to every thrust, all for real, but just as she liked to imagine it in her fantasies too. I couldn't hold myself, not after such a long build-up and the sheer thrill of her reaction to being spanked in front of strangers, and I'd barely got my pace up inside her before I felt myself start to come. When she masturbated over the fantasy, she liked to imagine me doing it all over her bottom as a final gesture of contempt for her in person and for traffic wardens in general, so that's what I did, spattering her reddened cheeks with drops of spunk.

She thought it was over, and reached back for her pussy to give herself what was obviously a desperately needed climax, but I caught her arms and twisted them up behind her back again. I had a little treat for her, something we'd discussed after the dogging incident but which had gone no further, and which she seemed to have forgotten about, because the expression on her face as I beckoned the watching men forwards was of pure horror.

The fight had gone out of her, though, and she accepted her fate with no more than a broken sob. The young man had been wanking and was ready for her, slipping it up while I held her over the bonnet, and she soon gave in completely, not even bothering to hide her pleasure as he jammed himself in and out of her. Like me, he came all over her bottom.

By that time the others were ready. They took turns with her, all three of them, and by the end she was a squirming, wriggling mess, her hat gone, her uniform jacket and blouse open with her bra pulled up to show her tits, her bottom plastered with spunk, and so dizzy she couldn't even focus. She did manage to masturbate, though, while the last of them was up her, mounted on her bum and pumping crazily into her pussy, and from the way she screamed I knew that I'd managed the perfect climax for her degradation.

Naturally it was all a set-up. Two of the men were old friends of mine and the third, the young one, was a porn actor I'd hired. We had a supposedly broken-down car blocking the lane too, to keep the chances of discovery to an absolute minimum. So yes, it was a fake, in a sense, but the important thing is that she didn't know that, while it also had the advantage that instead of making a run for it afterwards we all went for a fish supper in Cromer.

No doubt you're all thinking what an appalling sadist I am, and I admit it, but I do at least have the excuse that I switch roles and can therefore never be accused of dishing out what I'm not prepared to take. As we've said, a uniform allows you to express a role, both for yourself and for others. Wendy was as sweet as pie normally, but in her traffic warden's uniform she could be sneaky, vindictive and petulant, all characteristics that can lead a woman to being spanked.

Give a girl a different uniform and she can be a different person, and I don't just mean from my perspective. As you all obviously understand, wearing a uniform affects how you feel and therefore how you can behave, and each uniform brings its own characteristics. Some are limiting, others diverse. Whereas a traffic warden has quite a precise role, at least in my eyes, Wendy as a nurse can be a lot of things: dominant, submissive or just plain kinky. At the other end of the spectrum we have military uniforms, especially those with some rank, which exude authority. I'm not particularly submissive by nature, but give me a big strong woman in military uniform, such as a friend of mine called Marsha, and it makes me want to get down on my knees.

Marsha was one of the nicest women I've ever known: a good friend, a great cook and somebody I could really relax with. Unfortunately she also had the poor taste to marry a lawyer from Liverpool and I haven't seen her for years, although we were playing together right up to the week before her wedding.

Marsha used to like to dress as an army sergeant, and she really looked the part, nearly six feet tall, ramrod-straight and solidly built, with big hips and breasts that thrust out like a pair of cannon nozzles. Just to look at her like that was pretty terrifying, and to hear her bark out orders was enough to turn your spine to jelly. She loved to subdue men, and she was big enough and strong enough to do it for real a lot of the time. She knew about wrestling holds too, so once she had you pinned down you were genuinely helpless.

Once she got you pinned down – OK, once she'd got *me* pinned down, I admit it – she'd demand my submission, and if I didn't give it she'd sit her bum in my face until I gave in. She was a big girl, but she had a beautiful bottom, very full and firm, and she could fill a pair of men's green army fatigues to bursting point. Just that was an incredible experience, with her big round bottom straining out of her uniform trousers as she poised herself over my face, and it was easily enough to want to come over, but the real knack was to hold off until she did it bare.

That wasn't as easy as it sounds, because it hurts to have a fifteen-stone female army sergeant kneeling on your arms, believe me, and she'd never hurry it. She had her little ritual, you see, first trousers, then knickers, then bare, and she'd smother me and demand my submission each time, and only go further if I held off. I can be a stubborn so-and-so, and I knew that if I submitted too early she'd simply make herself comfortable on my face and bring herself off with her fingers, which was horribly frustrating with my arms pinned so that I couldn't get at myself. So I'd do my best, with her trouser seat right in my face so that I could barely breathe and her demanding that I slap my hand on the floor to show that I'd given in. If I twisted my head to the side she took it as a sign of submission too, so she was completely in control and I had no choice but to do it her way.

If I held off, and I didn't always, she'd eventually lift herself up, with her bottom poised a few inches above my face. Even before I'd got my breath back I'd be staring, and it was quite a sight, with her looming over me in her green jacket with the sergeant's stripes on her sleeves and her army cap on her unruly black curls, but most of my attention would be on the big green ball of her bottom as she unfastened her trousers and stuck her thumbs into the waistband. She'd make herself comfortable, check that she had me pinned down properly, then start to push her army trousers down.

She really did like to keep in role, and used to wear big plain knickers, usually black or white, but occasionally khaki or army green. Whatever colour they were, they would be stretched to bursting point across her bottom. No disrespect to slim girls, but there is something about a really big womanly bottom that sends the blood straight to my cock.

Once she'd got her trousers far enough down she'd demand my submission again, always asking three times before she put her bottom in my face. With just her knickers between us I would be well and truly smothered, the whole of my face immersed in bottom flesh and her cheeks half spread across my nose and mouth. It was a struggle to gulp in mouthfuls of pussy-scented air, and that was a big part of what always gave me an achingly hard erection without even touching myself.

She'd see, and laugh at me for my inability to control myself, but she'd never touch. Just occasionally, if she was in the mood, she'd unzip me and pull my pants down a little to leave my cock sticking out, but it was done more to humiliate me than for her pleasure, and certainly not for mine. She'd wriggle her bottom in my face too, to make herself more comfortable and get her cheeks as far apart as her knickers would permit, and once more demand my submission.

About half the time she'd get it, especially if she'd managed to get her bum so firmly in my face that I couldn't breathe at all. If so, she'd lift her weight a little and slip a hand down the front of her knickers, keeping me firmly pinned down while she masturbated herself to orgasm and rubbed her bum in my face. If not, she'd warn me that she was going to go bare and then lift up again.

I'd be put through the same ritual, with her thumbs stuck in the waistband of her knickers for a bit to really let what was about to be done to me sink in, then they'd come down and she'd be bare in my face. If she was a turn-on in knickers, then bare she was almost too much for me. She'd have her huge bottom naked and spread in my face, framed between her sergeant's jacket and her lowered army trousers and knickers. Her pussy would be open and wet, right over my mouth, and her bumhole showing between her cheeks so that when she sat down my nose would go in a little way.

Again she'd demand my submission, three times, but she'd never get it, not if I'd managed to hold off that long. My cock would be on the edge of explosion, and I'd know what was coming. She'd know I wouldn't give in, and that I wanted it, but she'd always give a little angry tut before she finally put her naked bottom in my face, and I think it did genuinely annoy her that it had got that far.

That never stopped her doing it. She'd reach back and spread her cheeks, holding them wide as she slowly lowered herself onto my face, usually with her pussy to my mouth, but if she was feeling particularly sadistic I'd get her bumhole instead and be made to kiss it before I started licking her. She'd make a last demand for my submission, and when I didn't give it she'd sit herself right down, smothering me completely in soft, cheeky bottom, and tell me that she wasn't going to get up until I'd made her come.

Even then she'd control it, wiggling her bottom in my face and sometimes even making me lick between her cheeks before she let me get my tongue to her clitoris, or even just rubbing herself off against my nose and mouth without bothering about my tongue at all. All the while I'd be rock-hard, but she'd never touch, not until she'd finished off in my face. When she had I'd finally get my treat, with her still sitting on my face, her bottom cheeks well spread, while she tossed me off with what I can only describe as contempt. By then I'd be in a state of complete submission to her, not to mention unable to breathe for my faceful of bum, which combined to produce some of the most intense orgasms of my life.

Marsha was delightful, and I do miss her. It's a rare treat to find a woman who enjoys sexual domination but can still respect a man after she's spent half an hour sitting on his face or had him over her knee for a spanking. Olivia was something of a contrast, a genuine female supremacist who had no respect for men anyway and viewed male sexuality as simultaneously amusing and somewhat disgusting, rather like somebody stepping in a cowpat.

I only played with her once, and frankly that was enough, but it was certainly interesting, and while I freely admit that she was absolutely in charge at the time I would also like to think that it was me who manipulated her rather than the other way around. But perhaps you should be the judges of that?

Oddly enough, I met her through Marsha, who must have passed on something of what the two of us got up to, but not in any great detail. For all her outward contempt, Olivia needed men to dominate, and on hearing how Marsha would deal with me she was keen to make my acquaintance. She also had a strong sense of honour and felt that it would be wrong to approach me while I was Marsha's creature, as she put it.

I first met her at Marsha's wedding, but it's a little difficult to negotiate highly perverse sexual encounters while seated around a table with an assortment of relatives, so very little was said. She did, however, manage to hint that I must be missing Marsha and seeking a replacement, which was true enough, and I therefore assumed that she would go in for the same sort of playful domination as her friend.

We exchanged numbers, but what with one thing and another I didn't get around to calling her immediately, and so was rather surprised to find a message on my answering machine demanding to know why I hadn't called and telling me I would be punished for my lapse. I took this as a piece of role play and rang her to apologise and hint that a little smothering might be in order. Like Marsha, she was a fairly well-built girl, and the thought of having her ample bottom lowered onto my face was more than a little appealing.

She had told me to come to a café in Edmonton, which I duly did, and I was pleasantly surprised to find her wearing a smart white-and-blue nurse's uniform, which suggested all sorts of interesting possibilities. I was somewhat disappointed to discover that she was a real nurse, a sister at the local hospital in fact, because I assumed that would mean she wasn't interested in the sexual possibilities of the uniform. By then I'd given myself away with a vengeance, but to my relief she simply put this down to further evidence of male crappiness.

Her actual needs were fairly straightforward. She wanted a male slave, somebody who would do the housework, act as occasional butler, cook and general dogsbody, for which she was prepared to reward me with privileges such as kissing her boots, being used as a footstool and, if I was very good, a spanking. If I was very bad I was to get the cane, a piece of logic I still don't fully understand.

Now I've no objection to taking a spanking from a woman, or even the cane, and I'd have been happy to worship her body, but at housework I draw the line. I was intending to make my excuses and leave at that point but, despite her dominant, even aggressive attitude, I came to realise that she actually needed me a great deal more than I needed her.

I therefore played up to my earlier mistake and claimed that I was only interested in submission to a nurse, even making up some entirely fanciful story about having been under the authority of a particularly stern matron while at school. What followed was a rather peculiar piece of negotiation, with her apparently in charge but with me steering things very much in my direction. I even managed to include the stipulation that I be made to come at the end of the session, and by that point she was sufficiently steamed up to accept.

We had agreed that she would come here directly after her shift finished on the Sunday, which meant she would arrive in the early afternoon. I was to be in bed, supposedly having called her out on false pretences, and she would then punish me for malingering. All the details of what she could and could not do had been worked out in advance, although unfortunately not as specifically as I might have wished.

It started beautifully. She looked exactly like what she was, a young sister from a large and busy hospital, and, if she was a little put out at being pushed into wearing her uniform to dominate me, then that only added to her brisk, stern manner. All I had to do was relax into the role, as she felt my pulse and took my temperature, all the while tutting and chiding me for my natural incompetence as a male.

She was moving a little faster than I might have hoped, and my cock had only begun to stiffen a little by the time she declared that I was perfectly well and had called her out for nothing, for which unpardonable sin she proposed to spank me. I assumed that was just eagerness on her part and allowed myself to be hauled out of bed and turned across her knee, all of which she did in a no-nonsense manner that I confess to finding extremely erotic.

Remembering how much I'd always enjoyed Wendy's protests and struggles, and keen to please my new playmate, I began to make a fuss when she told me I was to have my pyjamas taken down. Her response was to tell me to shut up and I was duly stripped, but there was nothing fake whatsoever about my further protests when she began to lay into my bottom and thighs. The hard swats, delivered to cold flesh, were far more painful than I was ready for.

Her response was wonderful. She stood up, tumbling me off her knee and onto the floor, reached up under her uniform skirt and, with a single irritable flourish, removed her underwear, a pair of large cream-coloured knickers which she proceeded to force into my mouth as I lay at her feet. Then it was back in position over her knee and the spanking began again.

This time I gritted my teeth and took it, or rather chewed on her knickers and took it. Before long she'd got me hot enough not to mind and I was lying very contentedly over her lap with my cock rubbing on the material of her nurse's uniform with every smack. Unfortunately this seemed to annoy her. She stopped, called me a dirty little boy and stated that sterner measures were in order, as she reached for the hairbrush I had foolishly left on my bedside table.

I hadn't said she could use a hairbrush, but I hadn't said she couldn't either, though had I known how much it hurt I'd definitely have banned it. Unfortunately, with my mouth full of her knickers there was nothing I could do to protest save make vague gulping noises, which were completely ineffectual. I got spanked, hard, so much so that when she finally stopped I was shaking uncontrollably and, to tell the truth, near to tears, although more of frustration than of pain. I also had an achingly hard cock.

What she did next was pure cruelty. I was far too high to resist, so made no complaint as she bundled me back onto the bed and used one of her stockings to tie her knickers in place inside my mouth and the other to secure my hands behind my back. She then rolled me over, with my erection sticking up out of my pyjama fly where the cord had snagged on it as they were pulled down.

I watched in fascination as she extracted a pair of rubber gloves from her bag and pulled them on, her face set in an expression of fastidious disdain. The gloves were followed by a tube of cream, which she squeezed onto my balls before taking me in hand. God, she was a cold bitch, showing no emotion beyond distaste as she manipulated my cock, with one finger up my bottom and her thumb pressed to my balls as she masturbated me.

I'm still not quite sure what she did inside me, but just as I was about to come she pressed the finger in my bottom, which brought me off with a violent wrenching sensation stronger than any orgasm I'd had before, although not as emotionally satisfying as the best with Wendy or Marsha.

Being used to women who expect a sex session to end with an orgasm each, I wasn't particularly surprised by what she'd done, only the way she'd done it, and I fully expected her to sit on my face for her own orgasm. That would have been fair enough, even though I'd only just come, but what I didn't realise was that she had made me come specifically so that I would get less pleasure and more torment out of what was to follow.

She had me helpless, remember, and I could only watch in horror as she extracted a large strap-on dildo from her bag. I never even got to see her naked, because she reached up under her skirt to put it on, showing as little flesh as possible, then rolled me face-down on the bed and pulled off my pyjama bottoms, which she fastened over my head. I knew I was going to be sodomised, and my buttocks were twitching badly as she climbed onto the bed and mounted me.

I felt the tip of the dildo press between my cheeks and I tried to resist, only to have her slip a hand down between my thighs and squeeze my balls, digging her nails in, so I soon gave in. Gay sex has never appealed to me, and even at public school I had managed to avoid the more or less obligatory buggerings, so I was effectively virgin. She had at least had the decency to open me up, but the sensation of having about eight inches of thick rubber cock pushed up my bottom was still almost more than I could take.

Not that I had the option. Up it went, with her sitting across my thighs so she could watch, and, after giving me a brief but stiff buggering, she began to rub herself on the base of the dildo. I have never felt so helpless in my life, or so used, tied down with a pair of knickers in my mouth as their owner sodomised me, but she had underestimated both my stamina and the depths of my perversity. Being buggered by a twelve-stone nurse in full uniform was just too good, too close to my most submissive fantasies, and by the time she was getting close to orgasm I was thoroughly enjoying the experience.

She came like that, gave me a few more strokes of the hairbrush while she lectured me on female supremacy and left. That really was the last straw, because I was still bound and gagged and it took the best part of an hour to get free. So you may imagine my astonishment when she called the next week to suggest a return match, only on her terms: no uniform, and I should pay for the privilege. I declined.

Six

'I knew somebody a bit like that,' Vanity put in as I finished, 'when I was at school.'

'Oh yes?' Cathy asked.

'She was our French teacher,' Vanity explained, 'and the officer in charge of the Combined Cadet Force, which meant navy as I was at Rollestone.'

'Rollestone?' John queried.

'It's a girls' school in Sussex,' Vanity explained, 'near Brighton. It was originally founded for the daughters of British naval officers and still has strong links with the navy.'

'Were you a cadet?' I asked.

'I was a cadet,' Vanity confirmed, 'which is how I picked up my taste for naval uniforms. I wasn't Vanity Belle then, just plain Jane Fox, and, believe me, I was a lot less confident than I am now.'

'I thought pupils from that sort of school were basically marriage fodder for the nobs and snobs?' Violet said. 'How did you end up doing burlesque?'

I'll tell you, but first you have to understand about Mademoiselle d'Arche, ex-ensign in the French Navy and more recently a teacher at Rollestone.

Even at eighteen, I should have realised that Mlle Enseigne d'Arche was a sadist. It was evident in her speech, her behaviour, her dress. She would take parade with a brisk vigour that had myself and every other cadet rigid with apprehension. A single perfectly chosen word could reduce a girl to tears, myself included, despite all the complicated, contradictory feelings her attitude evoked in me. The slightest scuff to a polished black shoe, the slightest crease to a mid-blue uniform shirt, and she would find it, her eye glinting with what in my innocence I took for military zeal but was in fact pure wickedness.

No doubt her background was above reproach, or she would hardly have been employed at Rollestone, but that didn't occur to us at the time. Rumours abounded: that she had been thrown out of the French Navy for having a lesbian affair, that she had been the mistress of a prominent official and had been paid off to prevent a scandal, that she had killed a lover and been forced to take a post at our remote English girls' school to avoid his vengeful relatives. None was true, or at least I very much doubt they were, but they served to provide her with a romantic, almost mystical allure that made everybody around her seem mundane. Or perhaps it was simply that I was in love with her.

One thing is for certain. By the time I was in the Upper Sixth and had been under her command once a week for three years I was so used to taking orders from her that it would never have occurred to me to do otherwise. I was completely under her spell, and, if my feelings included a touch of pique that I had not been promoted, then that only added to my desire to please her. It also inspired a peculiar emotion compounded of annoyance and a curious, somehow sexual weakness I found both disturbing and arousing.

I can still picture her as she was on that last day, at the passing-out parade in front of the assembled school and parents, in the same neat blue uniform as myself and the other cadets, but with her French ensign's insignia of double gold bars and an anchor, which she always wore despite being at a very British school. She was always immaculate, her black leather shoes polished to a gleaming brilliance, her stockings encasing her legs to smooth perfection, her blue-grey woollen skirt and jacket fitted perfectly to the contours of her hips and waist and bust, her pale-blue blouse and navy tie immaculate, her cap set on her head at exactly the correct angle.

Beyond her was the red-brick bulk of the school, set stark on the downs, its turrets and spires standing out against a sky of perfect eggshell blue, and beyond the school the darker, duller blue of the Channel, with a few whitecaps breaking well out to sea. The breeze was warm against my face, and a strand of hair had pulled loose from the tight bun we were obliged to wear on parade, tickling my forehead and nose. I dared not touch it, because I was at attention, and as Mlle d'Arche moved slowly down the line of girls I was dreading the inevitable put-down I would receive and already anticipating the stab of humiliation it would bring.

She reached me, her steel-grey eyes looking deep into mine, and her mouth twitched briefly at one corner, as if she was holding back a smile. My stomach was churning and I felt weak and out of control, but I remained perfectly still as she reached out one slim finger to tuck the escaped lock back into my hair. She barely touched me, yet her finger seemed to trace a line of fire across my forehead.

'You're a mess, Jane Fox,' she chided. 'What are you?'

'I'm a mess, Mam'selle Enseigne d'Arche,' I replied promptly.

129

Another girl somewhere along the rank tittered and I felt my humiliation swelling until I was sure I would wet myself.

'A disgrace,' she went on. 'A disgrace, a sloven, a slut. What are you?'

'A disgrace, a sloven and a slut,' I answered, resenting every word and yet utterly unable to deny her.

I knew I could have been strong. It was the last day, and the freedom of adulthood I'd longed for was just hours away. Some of my friends would have answered her back, others responded with dumb insolence. Not me. I repeated those awful words, shaming myself in front of them and her.

Had she spoken again I think I'd have begun to cry, but she knew when to stop and I was left blushing and trembling, reactions that must have been obvious to her. I felt tiny, weak and helpless but, most of all, humiliated, an emotion made a thousand times worse by the warm, moist sensation between my thighs.

The remainder of the parade, and of that day, is less clear in my memory, but far more so than the endless routine of the previous five years. My father was working as a consultant for a desalination plant in Saudi, which meant I would be staying an extra night before taking the train up to Gatwick the following afternoon. By teatime the school was almost empty, with all but a handful of the other girls gone and the staff too. It felt strange, with the classrooms and hallways empty and silent where they had always been full of noise.

I hadn't troubled to change out of my uniform, and in an effort to come to terms with my muddled feelings I retreated to my bedsit, intending to read. If the ground floor had felt empty, the bedsit passage felt abandoned. I was alone, the only sounds the faint sigh of the wind on the downs and the occasional cry of a seagull. For the next two or three hours I tried to concentrate on my book, a dog-eared Agatha Christie paperback, all the while trying to fight down the shameful need to touch myself between my legs. The second corpse had just been discovered when the silence was broken by the staccato clicking of heels on the wooden floor of the passage.

My immediate reaction was a guilty start, the result of years under the authority of mistresses who regarded reading alone in one's bedsit as evidence of laziness at the very least, and, although it no longer mattered, I found myself listening as the footsteps drew closer, hoping they would pass. When they came to a stop outside my door my heart gave a little involuntary jump, and again as a triple knock sounded on the wood, sharp and peremptory.

I had already guessed that my visitor was Mlle Enseigne d'Arche, simply from her manner, and found myself wondering what I'd done wrong, because I could think of no other reason she would wish to visit me. As I got to my feet I was wishing earnestly that I'd tidied my bedsit properly and finished my packing, but there was nothing I could do but invite her in. The door swung wide and there she stood, still in uniform, but to my surprise her voice was soft as she spoke to me, friendly, with a touch of uncertainty, quite different to what I was used to and had been expecting.

'I'm glad I caught you,' she said. 'I believe you're staying on another day?'

'Yes,' I confirmed. 'My flight leaves tomorrow evening.'

She came in and walked to the window, looking out across the grounds on which she'd been parading me just hours before. I waited, wondering why she seemed so hesitant, and at length she spoke again.

'Would you like to eat with me this evening, at my flat?'

My reaction was an overwhelming sense of gratitude. For years she had treated me as a clumsy, futile brat and the more she put me down the more I had looked up to her. There was a spark of rebellion deep within me, but that did no more than provide a stab of shame as I stammered out my answer.

'Please, yes, that would be very kind.'

'I thought we might,' she answered, 'as there's hardly anybody else in the school.'

'Thank you, yes. I just need to change . . .'

'Oh no, don't trouble to change. Come over now.'

She left, and I followed like a puppy at her heels. I remember watching her legs, the seams of her stockings running down from beneath her blue uniform skirt, across the gentle pits behind her knees and down her perfectly turned calves. Although I was in stay-ups myself, they were plain, and it never occurred to me that there might be any significance in her choice, let alone that such a thing might be related to her intentions towards me.

Her flat was at the far end of the main school buildings, where she was assistant mistress to one of the other houses. Each house was a little world unto itself, and there was a great deal of rivalry between them, so even in the sixth form it was unusual to visit another house. This one was now empty, and yet to be there still felt intrusive and a little mischievous, even with Mlle d'Arche as my sponsor.

I had never been in her flat before, although I knew it was a privilege occasionally extended to the senior cadets, and had always been piqued by my exclusion. It was everything I might have expected: neat, restrained and yet with touches of femininity and a subtly French style, all of which combined to increase my sense of awe until I hardly dared place one foot in front of the other on her immaculate carpet.

'Sit yourself down,' she offered. 'I'll pour us a glass of wine.'

'Wine?'

'Why not? Term ended at two o'clock this afternoon, since when you have no longer been a member of the school, and I have no longer been *in loco parentis*.'

'I suppose that's true, but . . .'

'You have drunk wine before, I take it?'

The familiar touch of derision was back in her voice, and I hastened to assure her that I had. It was true, in so far as I'd sneaked the occasional glass at home and for the last few months had been able to order in pubs, but that was the extent of my experience. Mlle d'Arche, I was sure, would be infinitely more sophisticated, in both her choice of wine and her presentation, so I was surprised when, instead of the elegant glass of some expensive white I had expected, she poured out a large goblet of strong red, from which she took a healthy swallow.

'That's better,' she said with a sigh, and smiled. 'I adore Provençe, don't you?'

I'd never been there, but I assured her I did. She didn't reply, leaving what to me was an embarrassed silence. I took a gulp of wine, imitating her, then ventured what I hoped was a sensible question.

'Is that where you're from?'

'No,' she answered. 'I was born in a village called Berneuse, near Chartres.'

'How wonderful!'

'No, it wasn't. It must be one of the dullest places on Earth. All everybody ever talks about is their families and their corn. I couldn't wait to get out.'

133

'Oh. Is that why you joined the navy?'

She nodded. We were getting near the territory of the rumours about her, and I wanted to know more but didn't dare ask for fear of offending her. She didn't seem inclined to go on either, and filled my glass before walking into the tiny kitchen off her living room.

'Come and talk to me while I cook,' she instructed, and I followed her in, wedging myself into a little alcove where a gable window looked out over the sea.

She cooked with the same brisk efficiency she brought to everything, preparing ingredients, juggling pans and talking all at once. I watched and talked. She made bouillabaisse, which seemed to me the peak of culinary refinement, although in the state I was in I'd probably have thought the same if she'd decided to serve beans on toast. For me, she could do no wrong, and so, when she at last asked what must have been a very carefully judged question, I fell straight into her trap.

We had finished both our food and the bottle of wine, after which she'd poured me a brandy. The conversation had come round to the cadets, something we had in common, so the question seemed a natural progression.

'Do you think I am a martinet?'

I didn't know what she meant, and found myself blushing as I confessed my ignorance.

'A martinet,' she explained, 'is any person in authority who is unreasonably strict with their charges.'

'No, no, not at all,' I replied hastily, thinking of what she'd called me that afternoon.

I was lying, and she knew it, lifting one quizzical eyebrow as she went on.

'No? I rather think you do, but you would be wrong. Strictness is essential in the military, as Jean Martinet knew.'

'Who was Jean Martinet?' I asked.

'Jean Martinet,' she went on, 'was Inspector General to the army of the Sun King, Louis Quatorze, and the first man to employ a standard system of discipline to turn recruits into fighting men. He also had an implement named after him, one of which I own. Would you like to see?'

'Yes, very much, thank you.'

I had no idea what she was talking about, and was expecting some piece of military paraphernalia, not the short-tailed whip she produced from a cupboard. It had a wooden handle and maybe a dozen leather thongs, each a foot or so long – a horrible thing, but the instant I saw it I was imagining her taking it to me. She must have judged me well, or needed me to the point of obsession beneath her cool exterior, because, although I was at least technically no longer under her charge, what she was said next would have been enough to get her sacked.

'Were I able,' she said, 'I would have taken this to your bottom this afternoon.'

'But I only had a little bit of hair out of place!' I answered.

It was, in effect, an admission of how I felt, although I didn't realise at the time. She did.

'So,' she said, 'had you been guilty of some worse misconduct you would not have considered it an unreasonable action for me to beat you?'

I must have said something, but I doubt it made any sense, while the heat in my face and my trembling fingers must have shown my reaction. She smiled.

'Stand up,' she told me.

I stood, unable to do otherwise, and turned my back to her, offering myself for all the resentment and fear and self-pity raging in my head. That act was my final undoing, and her smile grew broader as she flexed the whip in her hands.

'So you do want it?' she told me. 'I always thought you might. Stick out your bottom.'

Again I did as she asked, pushing out my bottom to round out the seat of my uniform skirt and present her with a target for the whip. I knew I was to be beaten, and I knew I wanted to be, but I didn't understand why, or why she would want to hurt me when I worshipped her. These tangled emotions had the first tears squeezing from my eyes even before she applied the whip.

It wasn't hard. If it had been, maybe I'd have broken and run. As it was I stayed put, the tears trickling slowly down my face as the martinet smacked down across my bottom. I could feel the weight of the thongs, heavy shocks becoming gradually harder, and with every one my emotions were driven higher. It didn't hurt, but it didn't have to. I was being beaten by Mlle Enseigne d'Arche, and to know that was more than enough. My helpless arousal built to overcome my shame and confusion. When it stopped, my overriding emotion was disappointment, then a sharp thrill as her fingers found the hem of my uniform skirt.

'I think, perhaps, your skirt needs to be lifted,' she told me, and I found myself nodding, too broken to resist, too excited to lie.

I hung my head, my vision hazy with tears, as she eased my skirt up, baring my thighs, exposing the tops of my stockings, the swell of my bottom cheeks and the seat of my knickers, to leave me vulnerable behind, shaking badly but ready for my punishment to go on. My skirt was tucked high, into its own waistband, as was the tail of my jacket, so that the full expanse of my panty seat was on show.

'That's much better,' she said, and once more the whip was applied to my bottom.

Now it stung, the thongs catching my flesh where it emerged from the leg holes of my knickers, and even across my seat, where I had only a thin layer of cotton to protect me. I was ready, though, more than ready, with a wonderful, unexpected warmth spreading through my bottom, and I was lost in a state of erotic worship for the woman who was beating me. She must have known she had me, but she took her time, applying another two dozen firm strokes across my seat before she once again stopped. This time I guessed what was going to happen. My knickers were coming down.

'We'd better get rid of these too, I think,' she said, and she pulled on my waistband.

I remember that detail, because knowing that she'd be able to see down the back of my knickers gave me a jolt of embarrassment like a miniature orgasm, and it happened again as they were peeled unceremoniously down off my bottom. She was very neat about it, inverting them around my thighs, just so, and spending a moment adjusting them to make sure there were no creases and perhaps to have a peep at what I was showing from behind. What a sight I must have looked too, an eighteen-year-old naval cadet bent over for punishment with my uniform skirt tucked up and my big green school knickers turned down to show my bottom, my bare cheeks red from the whip and the lips of my sex peeping out from between my thighs.

'That's better, isn't it?' she said, not a question but a plain statement of fact.

It was true. I did feel better, more exposed, more aroused, more alive. When she began to beat me again there was little left of the pretence that she was somehow giving me a long overdue punishment. She laid the strokes on, firm and even, across my bottom.

I was snivelling badly, with tears still streaming down my cheeks, but that was raw emotion, and I was gasping to every smack as well, not with pain. She could already have had me, if she had wanted to, taking advantage of the state she'd got me into to do with me as she pleased.

That was not her intention. She made a thorough job of me, cracking the martinet down across my cheeks with ever greater force, until at last I began to stamp my feet and jiggle my bottom in my mounting pain. I held my position, though, grasping my knees with my bottom stuck right out and everything showing to her, even the rude brown dimple between my cheeks.

I remember it all: her breathing, growing steadily heavier; my own gasps and cries as I was beaten; the crack of the martinet on my flesh; even the chime of the school bell to bring home the enormity of what was being done to me. And I remember my emotions, arousal and shame, resentment and gratitude, love and hate, all at once; and, most ridiculous and pathetic of all, a unique embarrassment at the possibility that she might be disgusted by the sight of my anus. Now I realise that she must have been thoroughly enjoying my exposure, especially that most humiliating detail, just as I do when I have some unfortunate little moppet bent over for the whip or cane.

When it finally stopped my entire bottom was burning and I was so excited that the juice was trickling down the insides of my thighs to wet my stockings and the gusset of my pulled-down panties. I thought it was over, and would no doubt have run back to my room to masturbate myself to orgasm even as I cried my feelings out into my pillow, but she had other ideas.

She sat down and put her arms out for me, cuddling me into her chest and stroking my hair, telling me to let my feelings out, which I did, clinging onto her body, shivering violently as the tears streamed down my face. She held me close, whispering to me and stroking me, with my face buried between her breasts so that I could feel the lace of her bra and the soft flesh beneath through her uniform blouse. I never even thought of pulling my knickers up to cover myself behind, and when she put a hand to the buttons of her blouse and started to undo them it seemed the most natural thing in the world.

'This will make it better,' she whispered as her blouse came wide, and the next moment she had lifted one breast free of her bra cup and fed her nipple into my mouth.

I sucked, feeding at her chest in a state of ecstasy beyond anything I could previously have imagined. She had me in a state of utter subjugation, suckling me with my smacked bottom stuck out behind, willing to do anything to please her, and she took full advantage. I was allowed to suckle both her breasts, which I genuinely thought of as a privilege, to make me better after my whipping, but I had no such illusions about what came next.

With both her nipples straining to erection and her blouse open across her chest, I was eased gently but firmly down to her sex. She held my hair while she adjusted herself, making very sure there was no escape for me as she rucked up her uniform skirt and eased aside the crotch of a pair of lacy black panties. Her sex lips were dark and puffy with excitement, open around a pink centre, to which she guided my head.

I was ordered to lick her and held in place while I did it, but neither was necessary. At that point I'd have done anything, because she had reduced me to a state that comes no other way but after a good beating from somebody in charge of me: not merely willing to please, but wanting to please, whatever it takes.

What it took was the application of my tongue to her sex while she twisted my hair in her fist and used the martinet on my bottom, all the while calling me a slut and a disgrace. She was only the third woman to come under my tongue, and she was the first to beat me, but I like to think I was good. I was certainly obedient. By the time she got there she was sighing with pleasure and rubbing herself in my face, and calling me her darling and her pet as well as a bitch and a slut.

Even when she'd finished it was not the end, far from it. She knew I was hers, and she knew we might very well never meet again, so she was determined to make the best of me. I was taken to bed, or at least to her bedroom, where we spent the rest of the night drinking brandy and playing together.

We talked too, and I learnt that she had wanted me more or less from the moment she had set eyes on me, but she had a strict rule of keeping her hands off her charges. I admitted I'd felt much the same for her, and after that things changed, with more kisses and gentle touches replacing the urgent sadism of before. Sometime around dawn she at last returned the favour I had been made to give so often, having me lie back on her bed as she climbed on top to press her mouth to my sex while I did the same for her. As I clung to her with my body tight in an orgasm that felt as if it would never end, I achieved a desire that had been growing within me for years, and has never dulled.

I never saw Mlle Enseigne d'Arche again, but from that day onwards sex became inextricably linked with being in uniform, and with other women. To this day I've never had a man, or felt any attraction to men, which is one reason I kept my show more toned down this evening. Had the audience been exclusively female it would have been a different matter. After the way she treated me, you might also expect me to have become fixated on submission and punishment, but I didn't.

It was all about rank for me, and authority. Mlle Enseigne d'Arche had both, and so it was only natural that I submit to her rather than the other way around, but I would love to have been promoted. Had I been, I like to think I might have taken one of my friends to bed and given her much the same treatment as Mlle Enseigne d'Arche gave me, although the truth is I'd never have had the confidence to do it, not the same way.

The next couple of years were more frustrating than anything else. There was nothing for me in the tiny community of foreign workers in Saudi, or in the country as a whole. With no other input for my sexuality I became ever more fixated on my one exquisite experience and everything it involved. I used to lie on my bed and spank myself with a fly swat until I'd achieved that same wonderful glow she'd given me with the martinet, and then masturbate as I imagined myself back in her flat with my bottom hot and my face buried between her thighs. It was never fully satisfying, though. I didn't have her and I didn't have my uniform.

By the time my father's contract had run its course I was twenty. We returned to England and I immediately applied to join the Royal Navy, but was turned down on medical grounds. That was a blow to me at the time, although with hindsight it was probably for the best. After all, my motives centred on first allowing myself to be made the plaything of a senior female officer and later finding somebody I could punish and humiliate myself, which are hardly the ambitions they look for.

It had never occurred to me that I might be rejected, and so it left me not only depressed but at a loose end. I considered teaching, but quickly rejected the idea because, while I knew my intentions would be moral, I wasn't at all sure I had the strength to hold back as Mlle Enseigne d'Arche had done. This was also shortly after they'd changed the law to make it illegal to take advantage of anyone in your care, regardless of age, and I had no desire to get locked up.

My next experience was completely unexpected. While I'd accepted that I was a lesbian, I had tried to rid myself of my obsession with naval uniform, because it seemed likely to do me a lot more harm than good. I even went to a therapist, but the view of what was 'normal' she held out to me depressed me even more, and had the opposite effect, making me feel that the possibility of realising my desire was the only thing worth living for.

Oddly enough, that gave me a lot more energy and drive, so I suppose you could say she succeeded, only not in the way she intended to. With my accent and background and, let's be honest about it, my looks, it wasn't hard to get a job as a diplomatic translator, which was quite well paid and also interesting. I got a flat of my own too, which meant that for the first time I had real privacy, and could dress up without having to worry about making embarrassed explanations to my parents.

Just to think of being in uniform again was enough to make me hot and dizzy, so much so that issues of reality didn't come into it. Also I could choose the smartest possible dress uniform rather than have to settle for whatever was worn by the unit I'd joined. Despite having all the choice in the world, my first thought was to go for the same smart navy blues I'd worn as a cadet at Rollestone.

They were relatively easy to get hold of, although it would be far easier for men, so much so that I almost got into cross dressing before I finally managed to find the real thing at an army surplus store just off the Euston Road. It was a little big for me, and needed taking in, but I didn't mind that at all, not when it had the single gold bar of a sub-lieutenant.

Most people wouldn't even understand that, or they'd think I was a geek as well as a pervert, but just the word sub-lieutenant was enough to make me wet. The implication that I might be in authority or subject to authority, and therefore might equally well give or receive punishment, was exactly in tune with the fantasies I'd been building up in my head for so long. I imagine the woman in the shop thought I was mad or ill, because I couldn't stop my hands trembling just from the touch of the fabric.

I wanted to find somewhere private and hold the uniform to my face while I masturbated, but I knew that the longer I took the better it would be in the end. First I needed to complete the uniform, and fortunately I could get a plain blue blouse and the right tie then and there. Also, and much more importantly, it came with the correct cap. Smart black hold-ups were easy, and I already had proper shoes, which only left my underwear. I know that might not seem part of the uniform, but it was important to me.

My first thought was to go for big green school knickers like the ones I'd worn on that glorious night with Mlle Enseigne d'Arche, but they didn't seem right for a sub-lieutenant. Her own had been black and lacy, and that seemed far more appropriate, whether I was to have them taken down to have my bottom welted or after I'd given the same treatment to some hapless subordinate. I treated myself to a pair of French knickers in black silk, with a bra to match, which felt very refined and just the sort of thing a junior officer should wear.

Dressing up was an act of masturbation in itself. You all put your uniforms on and disarrange them for excitement, but I get mine from dressing, even the underwear when I know my uniform is going on top. It took all my willpower to make the adjustments first, but I managed it, then turned my phone off and locked the door before setting out my uniform and underwear on my bed.

Just sliding the silky knickers up around my hips and feeling their smooth texture on the flesh of my bottom and sex was exquisite, as was the touch of my bra as it took up the weight of my breasts and the way the lace trim tickled my nipples. Next came my stockings, each one rolled slowly up my leg, and I was ready for the main act.

I put on my blouse with my eyes closed, imagining I was back at Rollestone as I went through the ritual of doing up the buttons. My tie followed, checked in the mirror to make sure it was exactly right, then my shoes, but I wanted to leave the most important part until last. I put my hair up and sat my cap on top of it, then my jacket, slipping each trembling arm inside to leave me with hot shivers of excitement running through my body.

Last came my skirt, eased up my legs and over my hips, to fit just so, snug around my bottom and tummy and thighs. That was too much for me, to feel that familiar weight and texture, just as it had been when I'd pushed out my bottom for Mlle Enseigne d'Arche to take her martinet to my cheeks. I closed my eyes again and held the pose, wishing she was there to beat me, strip my bottom and beat me again, then to hold me trembling in her arms and suckle me at her breast.

That I couldn't do it really hurt, and yet I couldn't help myself. I was sobbing as I collapsed back on the bed, but that didn't stop me getting on all fours and tucking my uniform skirt up into its own waistband, just as she had done to me. My bottom felt soft and peculiarly sensitive in my hands as I kneaded my flesh, and deliciously exposed once I'd pushed down my knickers to go bare.

My eyes were still shut, but I could picture myself perfectly, a smart young sub-lieutenant ready for discipline, her bottom bare to whatever ranking officer was about to apply a cat-o'-nine-tails to her shrinking flesh, scared yet contrite, fearful yet accepting the need for her beating. I knew then that I would have to make a cat for myself, and for others, but the thought stayed in my head only a moment before I'd reached around under my bottom to get at my sex.

I began to tickle myself towards orgasm, imagining Mlle Enseigne d'Arche watching me, or making me do it to myself while I licked her, remembering the feel of the martinet across my flesh and of her nipple in my mouth, the taste of her pussy, but most of all how she had looked in her immaculate uniform, holding the whip as she talked me into accepting my first and only proper punishment. There were tears in my eyes as I came, and I dropped down very quickly from my high, leaving me promising myself I would find somebody to share my feelings with if it was the last thing I did.

145

My first thought was the Internet, which I'd only just got, but I was still very embarrassed to admit to my needs and wary of meeting strangers. I took it slowly, and something happened before I'd plucked up the courage to meet anybody. Most of the people I knew in London were old school friends, and I'd occasionally get invited to a party or dinner. One came up which was fancy dress, the twenty-first birthday party of a girl who'd been very much the social focus of her year at school and seemed determined to continue her dominance into adult life.

She'd been one of those pushy, assertive girls who always knew what she wanted and generally got it, and as a woman she was, if anything, worse. In fact, the night before the party I allowed myself a little fantasy in which it turned out that all my friends knew about Mlle Enseigne d'Arche and that she had arranged for me to be flogged in my uniform as part of the entertainment. I don't suppose anything of the sort ever entered her head, but it was nice.

What happened was almost the exact opposite. I went in my uniform, sure that it would be thought an amusing gesture rather than weird, but was expecting a night of chatting with old friends and nothing more. That was how it started, but a lot of the girls were intent on their partners and men in general, which bored me, so I quickly found myself gravitating towards those who were on their own and single.

One of them was a girl two years younger than me, the hostess's little sister, Ophelia. You'd have expected her to have at least a dozen men flocking around her, but she seemed far more interested in talking to me. She'd been in a different house to me at school, and what with the age gap I only really remembered her as a face in the crowd, but of course we had a great deal in common – including Mlle Enseigne d'Arche.

By now we were both quite drunk, and it occurred to me that what Mlle Enseigne d'Arche had done to me she might also have done to other girls. We began to talk about how strict it had been in cadets, and before long I was nearly certain that Ophelia was fishing for confessions from me just as I was fishing for confessions from her. The thought of her having shared the same experience was exciting, but the possibility that she might want to repeat it with me was agonising. I had to phrase the question carefully to allow me to back-pedal if necessary.

'Did she ever introduce you to Jean Martinet?'

My heart was in my mouth as I said it, and I knew the answer even before Ophelia spoke. Her eyes were glistening and a blush had begun to creep up from her chest, where most of her breasts showed over the top of the tiny pirate costume she was wearing.

'Yes,' she told me, 'and you?'

'Yes. I . . . I rather enjoyed it, actually.'

She giggled, and after that there was no doubt about what was going to happen. The party was at her parents' house, a mansion on the borders of Surrey with three storeys and something like twelve bedrooms. We flirted a little more and then slipped upstairs when nobody was looking, to her bedroom. The moment the door was closed we were in each other's arms.

There has always been a delicious sense of the forbidden about the first kiss with another girl, and this time was no different. With Ophelia's mouth open under mine and knowing we had both tasted Mlle Enseigne d'Arche's martinet, my excitement was so great that it took all my willpower not to simply tumble her onto the bed and let desire take over. I wish we had now, and saved our less straightforward needs for another day, but I was in my uniform, and

I wanted to make use of it. With her as my junior and in her silly pirate outfit there was no question of who was in charge: Sub-Lieutenant Fox.

'I don't think this is quite the time for that sort of behaviour,' I told her, pulling away. 'Do you, Brooke?'

It took her all of a second to fall into role.

'No, Miss,' she said, stepping back and coming to attention.

'And why are you dressed like that?' I demanded.

'Fancy-dress party, Miss,' she answered.

'That's no excuse. It's slovenly. Take it off. Everything.'

I wasn't as good as Mlle Enseigne d'Arche, nor as calm. I couldn't be, not when I needed Ophelia so desperately. The pirate costume had to come off anyway. It broke the mood, and, as she presumably didn't have a uniform, she'd have to be nude. I watched her undress, trying to seem cool and dispassionate but sure she could hear the thudding of my heart. She was small and very compact, with beautiful smooth skin and a lovely roundness to her figure, her bottom especially. I made her show it to me.

She was so obviously aroused, with her nipples standing to attention and the scent of her sex heavy in the air, and yet she was still flushed with embarrassment at being naked in front of me. I made her do drill, just as Mlle Enseigne d'Arche had drilled both of us, moving between attention and at ease, saluting in different ways, marching on the spot, and with each hesitation I would slap her bottom with the tips of my fingers. Every touch of her flesh sent a shock through me, and I was finding it harder and harder to keep control, yet I was determined to put her through her paces before we simply gave in to each other.

The party was forgotten, her room a little private world where I could parade her naked and enjoy the authority of my rank. I made her do handstands and touch her toes, and the sight and smell of her bare, wet sex again came close to making me lose control. I had to punish her, and quickly, then put her down on me.

'You're not good enough,' I snapped. 'In fact, you're a sloven, a disgrace, a slut.'

She shivered at the echo of Mlle Enseigne d'Arche's words, making the flesh of her breasts and bottom shake.

'You should be whipped,' I told her. 'Fifty strokes of the cat, in front of the rest of the cadets. But, as it is, I shall spank you. Come here.'

I had nothing to hand to beat her with properly, but I wanted the intimacy of her body against mine and my hand on her flesh. She felt warm and soft as she laid herself across my lap and lifted her bottom into spanking position. I could feel her breathing, low and hard, and she was shaking as she readied herself for spanking, naked over her lieutenant's knee, and me without a stitch out of place.

I tried to make it a punishment, slapping hard to make her cheeks quiver and draw squeaks from her mouth, but the need to touch her was too much for me. Soon I was stroking her cheeks between smacks, then between them, teasing her bottom hole and the lips of her sex, until she'd begun to moan and push her hips up for more. At last I could hold back no longer.

'You are a dirty little pig,' I told her, 'and as you seem incapable of acting like a lady I shall treat you as the slut you are. Come here.'

Mlle Enseigne d'Arche would have put her on her knees to lick, cool and dominant in her immaculate uniform with Ophelia grovelling naked and spanked at her feet. I didn't have the discipline, but simply rolled back onto the bad and hauled her on top of me. She didn't need telling what to do, tugging my uniform skirt up, pulling my knickers aside and burying her face in my sex. Her bottom was right in front of me, and I continued to spank her as I licked, still wanting to punish her even as we made each other come.

It wasn't going to take me long, and as she licked me I could feel the years of frustration boiling up inside me, so there was as much emotion as physical pleasure in what I knew would be the orgasm of a lifetime. She was getting close too, wriggling her bottom in my face with her hands clutched tight to my raised thighs as she licked. I was spanking as hard as I could, slapping her cheeks turn and turn about, to make them part and show off between, with her tiny pink bottom hole winking as we started to come – which was the sight that greeted her sister as the door opened.

I won't describe the hysterics, the accusations and recriminations, the way Ophelia was treated as if she was suffering from some kind of mental disability, and how I was ostracised by all but a handful of my old friends. Suffice to say that it was deeply hurtful, and that knowing how hypocritical some of them were being was no help at all. Maybe I should have been stronger and faced them down, but it was so much easier to run.

So that was the end of that, and for the second time in my life I tried to rid myself of my compulsion, this time seeking fully qualified psychiatric help instead of a largely self-proclaimed therapist. I told him everything about Mlle Enseigne d'Arche and Ophelia, and he listened patiently and tried to help, but ended up suggesting medication. Maybe I'm old-fashioned, but I always remember what my grandmother said a few weeks before she died after being put on medication, that once the quacks get hold of you they never let go. I never collected my prescription.

Fortunately there was no connection between my job and my old school friends, so I was still earning and it wasn't that long before I began to get over the shock of what had happened with Ophelia. By the way, although that was a really horrible experience, if we hadn't been caught it would have been a beautiful one, and wouldn't have done anyone any harm at all.

It was nearly three months before I tried my uniform on again, but the incident had spoilt it for me. I could start off, enjoying being dressed up and imagining either being in deep trouble with a superior officer or putting some pretty cadet through her paces, but, as soon as I began to masturbate, the images in my head would slip to the outraged face of Ophelia's sister.

I hoped the problem would pass, but it didn't, and by the time I hadn't been able to come for six months I was getting desperate. Trying to focus on anything other than my uniform fantasy was hopeless, and my one attempt at visiting an ordinary lesbian bar was a disaster because I couldn't help but see disapproval in every face. In the end I decided to try a different uniform, and to my surprise it worked.

It had to be military, there was never any doubt about that. There were some beautiful army uniforms which I'd focused on but never considered buying because I was so fixed on Mlle Enseigne d'Arche and my naval fantasy. My favourite, in that it is quite simply the smartest uniform ever created, was the black SS outfit, but I was certain that anybody who saw me in one would automatically assume it was a reflection of my politics, so I never found the courage to get one.

There are other smart black uniforms, especially Russian ones for submarine crews and police, but I quickly found that too many people associate them with Nazism without bothering to check the specific insignia. Airforce blues are good, but too close to my naval outfit for comfort, while I've never really liked green. It's not my colour, and somehow it seems grubby, even when brand new. Brown is worse, and, while I did come across one rather snappy red outfit, it made me look like a lift attendant.

I'd already looked at US Navy uniforms, but dismissed them as too similar to our own, until I discovered that there's also a female white dress uniform, which is what I've got on, and it's gorgeous. Admittedly I've put a couple of small tucks in the waist to make the line even smarter than it already was, but that's all. You can get them mail order for a couple of hundred pounds. I was even able to give myself an instant promotion, mainly because two gold stripes are smarter than one, but also because after spanking Ophelia I'd decided that I took more pleasure in giving than receiving.

Ironically, that got me into trouble and earned me my last punishment, which I'll tell you about, but let me fill you in first. I fell in love with my dress whites at first sight and ordered them over the net, because judging by what seeing a mannequin dressed in them could do for me I was pretty sure they'd get me over my mental block.

I was right, because no sooner had they arrived than I knew I could do it. As always I took my time, choosing a quiet moment, late at night, and laying out everything I needed before getting dressed. I showered and came into my bedroom naked so that what I was doing seemed completely fresh. This time I put my stockings on first, then a lacy white bra and panties set I'd also ordered from the States, because when I do something I like to do it properly.

Inevitably my mind turned to Ophelia, but I had known it would be impossible to keep her out of my head. I kept going anyway, slipping into my fresh white blouse and fastening my navy-blue cravat, sliding my skirt up over my hips and fastening it in place, pushing my feet into my shoes. The jacket was a beautiful fit, snug to my hips but accentuating my waist and the line of my breasts and shoulders, while the twin stripes on each sleeve and the row of gold buttons down the front looked incomparably smart.

My cap was the perfect finishing touch, leaving me as a young, feisty US Navy lieutenant, ready for action. Not that I intended to fight anybody, except in the confines of my head. My body already felt warm, and after a while inspecting myself in the mirror I got down to business, deliberately playing through the scene with Ophelia in my mind, the urgency of her kisses, her neat, compact body as she undressed, her surrender as she crawled across my knee for her spanking, the excitement of holding her nude in my arms as we licked each other.

And her sister, always her wretched sister, whom I'm not even going to dignify with her own name. We'll call her the Brat. So many times my fantasy had broken when the Brat caught us, but not this time. I imagined how I should have reacted, facing her down and dragging her into the room, jamming her little sister's knickers into her mouth to shut her up, hauling her across my knee and spanking the living daylights out of her for being a prissy, stuck-up, judgemental, manipulative, evil-minded, moronic bitch.

By then I was on the bed, my eyes tight shut and my uniform skirt rucked up to my waist to let me get at my sex. I'd been expecting the orgasm to end all orgasms, after so long going without, but there was more vengeance than ecstasy in my mind as I came, and I was left triumphant but not fully satisfied. The uniform was good, though, and it's been my favourite ever since.

I was going to tell you how it got me into trouble. After the incident with Ophelia and the Brat I had a lot of time on my hands, and my attitude had become considerably more bolshie. It's very easy, when you've been to a school like Rollestone, to stick with your old friends, and to be truthful the sense of social superiority it gives is very satisfying and can provide a cocoon against the outside world and all its unpleasantness. Some Rollestone girls never leave that cocoon.

The Brat had made very sure I did, and, as I'm sure many of you know, it's a horrible sensation when you're the focus of everybody's disapproval and prurient interest at the same time. I had to get out, and the only company I felt I could bear was that of my fellow lesbians, even if they were vanilla. So I started going to bars and searching the net again, more thoroughly this time, but I'm not particularly good with strangers and, what with shyness, uncertainty and my accent, it took me a long time to get accepted.

I had found one bar, in Soho, where uniforms were accepted, if only because they were no more unusual or provocative that what a lot of the other girls wore. It took me a while to pluck up the courage to go there, but I had to show off my new dress whites, and Whispers was the only place to go. As it happened, I needn't have worried at all. I was not merely accepted, but lionised, with everybody saying how smart I looked and eager to talk to me, so that after several glasses of wine it looked very likely that I'd be going home with somebody.

You know how it is sometimes, though: when you're spoilt for choice you tend to go for the toughest option. None of my admirers was in uniform, but one other girl was, a tall, lean, blonde with cropped hair and exactly the sort of jet-black uniform I'd never dared to wear. She had the double stripe of white piping on her shoulder tabs, which to my way of thinking made her my junior and a candidate for a bit of drill followed by a spanking.

I admit I was showing off to my new friends as I walked across to the blonde, and I admit suggesting her boots weren't properly polished wasn't the best of introductions, but I still say her reaction was excessive. She turned to look at me, downwards because she was at least half a head taller than I am, first in amazement, then in anger. I realised I'd made a mistake and was about to apologise, but I never got the words out.

She grabbed me by the wrist, twisted my arm behind my back and frogmarched me into a sort of backroom, much to the amusement of everyone else, including my new-found admirers. They all crowded in behind us too, and watched as I was bundled over the tall girl's knee, my immaculate white uniform skirt turned up, my sassy white panties taken down and my bare bottom smacked.

It was so sudden I hadn't had a chance to get my head around it. I fought for real, but she was horribly strong and it did me no good at all, while I lost my dignity from the first slap, kicking and wriggling about to the sound of laughter and rude suggestions from the girls who a moment before had been almost worshipful in their attention.

That was a long spanking, and a hard one. It was hideously shameful too, with my bottom bare and my sex on show to a couple of dozen laughing girls, while my cap fell off and my hair was soon in disarray, which was almost as shameful as knowing how much they could see. I'm afraid I squealed rather a lot too, and by the time she'd finished with me and I'd finally managed to get up off the floor I was burning with embarrassment.

As you can imagine, that did not do a lot for my sense of authority, but it was exactly the sort of behaviour I'd been hoping for, only of course not with me on the receiving end. She'd got me completely off balance, and when she took me by the ear and led me into the loos I went like a lamb, not sure what she was going to do to me or whether I wanted it or not.

She made me lick her, on my knees in a lavatory cubicle, an unspeakably sordid thing to do, maybe, but the contrast between my perfect uniform, her own black one and what she was making me do was so strong, and so in tune with my fantasies, that I just couldn't help myself. I made myself come, then and there, with one hand between my legs as I licked her sex with my head trapped up her uniform skirt and my own lifted to show off my red bottom behind. Now that was an orgasm like no other.

I wasn't exactly happy about it afterwards, but it was what I'd wanted, in a sense, and so I put a brave face on it, apologising to her and buying her a drink. That was my salvation. After that I was one of them, and it wasn't long after that when I met Kitten, at the same place. As she has no shame whatsoever I'll tell you about that too.

The moment I saw her I wanted to take her to bed, and I remember exactly how she looked. She was at the bar in Whispers, sitting on a high stool in a pure-white nurse's uniform, the real thing, including her cap, although she looked anything but demure. She had one leg up on the strut of a neighbouring stool, and black stockings on, showing off the shape of her calf, while her skirt had ridden up enough to expose quite a lot of thigh. Her shoes were black, shiny patent leather, with a couple of inches of heel, very smart and yet still practical. She had her hair up, although a couple of wisps had escaped and hung down to one side of her face, and she was wearing vermilion lipstick and sucking a drink through a black straw. I wanted to punish her immediately, and more.

What I didn't know, at the time, was that her reaction to me was almost exactly the same. There's nothing easier than making a move on a girl when she's as keen as you are, and at the end of the evening we went home together. I knew what I wanted, and so did she, but unfortunately it was the same thing, and, while that's fine if you're vanilla, it's not when you're kinky.

As the cab wound its way through Islington towards her flat, I was wondering if I should make her do drill for a while and then perhaps have her touch her toes for the strap or cane, or whether it would be better to treat her as my blonde had treated me and spank her out of hand. In the end I decided to take it slowly, and to start by allowing her to serve me, which conjured up an enticing image of her in her pretty white nurse's uniform. You can imagine my shock, then, at her first words, uttered before she'd even closed the door properly behind us.

'Get in the bathroom and pop your panties off. I think I'll give you an enema first.'

I'd never connected enemas with sex up until that point, so there was a moment of complete disorientation while I wondered why she wanted to stick a hose up my bottom, but I rallied pretty quickly, taking her chin in my hand and looking into her eyes as I answered.

'I see you need to learn a little respect for your superiors, nurse. You get into the bathroom, and you "pop your panties off", while I find something to put across your bottom.'

She didn't answer immediately, taken by surprise, but pulled my arm down first and spoke in her normal voice.

'Hang on. I heard you took a spanking the other week, in front of everybody.'

'That's right,' I admitted, 'and it's about time I worked that out of my system, on you.'

'Oh, yes? That I'd like to see!'

'You will.'

We were both smiling, but neither of us was going to back down, especially me, as I had a nasty suspicion that if I gave in I would end up with the threatened spanking as well as the enema hose up my bottom. I'm bigger than her, but not by much, and I backed cautiously into her living room, waiting my chance to get to grips with her. She moved first, grabbing me around the waist and trying to trip me up at the same time, but I held on and we went down together, onto the thick rug in the middle of the room.

I suppose we're about as strong as each other, but I was determined to win, and I had the thought of that hose being inserted up my bottom to spur me on. She put up a good fight, but before too long I had her face-down on the rug and was sitting astride her back with her arms pinned under my legs. I was gasping for breath, my hat had come off and she'd pulled my hair out of its bun, but I was triumphant as I spoke to her.

'Now let's see who's going to take a spanking!'

Her response was to try to buck me off her back, but I was ready for that and held my place, with her struggling underneath me, and even managed to turn around so that I was facing her bottom and legs. As I realised that I had her well and truly helpless I wanted to laugh, but held my poise, every bit the cool and collected officer. She stopped, and I began to inch her uniform up, deliberately slowly.

'I think I'll have you bare for a start,' I told her as the tops of her stockings came on show, 'and do stop struggling, or you'll only make it worse for yourself.'

'You're the one who's making it worse for yourself, you bitch!' she spat. 'You wait!'

'Temper, temper, Kitten,' I chided as I tucked her skirt up under my thighs to leave the seat of her black cotton knickers on show. 'Wouldn't it be best to take what you deserve with a little more dignity?'

'Fuck off! I mean it, Jane, if you don't stop now I'll get you, and I'll tie you up and leave you until you wet yourself. I'll piss in your mouth and all over your pretty uniform! No! Just fuck off! You bitch!'

Her last outburst was because I'd pulled her knickers down, baring a round, cheeky bottom to the room. She began to fight again, kicking her legs up and down and making her bottom quiver like a jelly, which was so funny I couldn't hold my laughter in any more.

'Bitch!' she repeated.

'Oh, come on, Kitten,' I answered. 'You'd have done this to me and worse, wouldn't you? So it's only fair.'

Her answer was an angry grunt, but as I put one hand to a fleshy bottom cheek and gave it a wobble she spoke again.

'OK, OK, spank me, but I warn you, you'll get ten times what you dish out!'

'If you can subdue me, fair enough,' I told her, and I meant it. 'But none of your dirty stuff, OK? I'm not into watersports.'

She spat an answer, but I didn't catch it. I was having too much fun with her bum, wobbling her cheeks and spanking her gently to send little shivers through her flesh. You do have the most gorgeous bottom, Kitten. I never cease to be amazed at how such a slim girl can hold up so much meat, and you should hardly be surprised that everyone wants to spank you. It's inevitable.

I meant to punish her, for just looking the way she did, but for what she'd threatened to do to me as well. But, as with Ophelia, the temptation to just let myself go and bury my face between her bottom cheeks was hard to resist. Nevertheless, I did, first spanking her by hand, until her cheeks had begun to glow and her furious silence had given way to little sobs and moans, then using her own shoe on her for a proper beating.

It must have hurt, because she was squealing and struggling at first, but then she gave in, and was begging me to stop instead of calling me a bitch and threatening me. The strange thing was, the harder I beat her the less she complained, until she began to push her bottom up for more and wriggle herself against the rug.

'You're nothing but a slut, Kitten,' I told her, and stopped. 'Now roll over.'

She obeyed without hesitation, and there was no resistance at all as I moved back a little and settled myself over her head. I wanted to put my bottom in her face, but even then it seemed rather a liberty, to queen her when we'd only just met. So I sat down still clothed, with the seat of my uniform skirt against her face, and rolled her legs up, twisting her knickers around her ankles to hold them in place, and tugged her uniform up to get her properly bare.

That's the great thing about real uniforms. No little rubber number could have looked even close, and as I started to spank her again I could picture exactly how we would look. There I was, immaculate in my dress whites, and I'd even put my hat back on, seated on her face, a navy lieutenant dishing out a punishment to a recalcitrant nurse who'd had to have her face sat on to subdue her and was now rolled up, her skirt tucked up out of the way, her knickers around her ankles and her bottom flaunted with her sex and anus on full view as she was spanked with her own shoe.

I was thoroughly enjoying myself, and from the way she kept nuzzling the seat of my skirt I knew I could take the little slut further. As always, I did it slowly, raising my bottom and pulling up my skirt very gradually so that what was about to be done to her could really sink in. I was in a thoroughly sadistic mood too, and eager for revenge for the sheer cheek of what she'd threatened to do to me.

'Well, you wanted to put a tube up my bottom,' I told her as I pushed my knickers down, 'so how about your tongue up it instead?'

With that I sat on her face, bare. I'd expected resistance, but her tongue went straight to my bottom hole, and I know it's a filthy thing to do but, believe me, if you haven't made anybody do it to you, make sure you do, because it feels exquisite. It's wonderful to know you're making somebody do it too, as part of a punishment, especially with Miss Nursey here.

I came like that, queened on her face in her smart little uniform while she rubbed herself over what I was doing to her, and this time it was quite simply the

161

perfect climax, long and hard, and all the while with my image of myself as Sub-Lieutenant Fox fixed firmly in my head. And the rest, as they say, is history. Kitten and I have been playmates ever since; she got me onto the burlesque circuit, which gives me the perfect opportunity to dress up in uniform. I took Vanity Belle as my stage name, and here I am.

Seven

'Did you get your own back, Kitten?' Cathy asked.

'Count on it,' Kitten answered, throwing Vanity a dirty look, 'and, believe me, she gives in a lot more easily than I do.'

'When I choose to,' Vanity answered.

I glanced from one to the other, wondering, if they might not be about to end up in a tangle on the floor and, if they did, which one of them I'd like to lose. It had to be Vanity. Kitten had gone down to her underwear, which left very little to the imagination, but Vanity hadn't provided so much as a glimpse of thigh. Furthermore, while her story had me as hard as before, it was plain that I had no chance at all of sampling her wares.

Kitten, I think, might have done it, but Vanity quickly changed the topic of conversation, addressing Cathy.

'So what about you? You seem so quiet and shy. Did Richard make you dress like that?'

'No,' Cathy answered, and hesitated before continuing with greater confidence. 'I like to role play school, but I've always kept work and pleasure separate, until tonight, because Richard asked us to come in uniform and I like being a schoolgirl.'

'How do you mean, you role play school?' Paul asked.

'I belong to a society that recreates old-fashioned school scenarios,' Cathy explained.

'With spanking?' Kitten demanded.

'The society is called the London Disciplinary School,' Cathy told her, 'so yes, with spanking. Let me explain.'

The LDS was set up for people who like the idea of being in an old-fashioned school, like in the 30s or 50s maybe, which you probably think means it's full of old men trying to take a nostalgia trip, but that's not it at all. You'd be amazed at how many young people, women as well as men, are into it. Or maybe you wouldn't, especially you, Vanity.

This idea that wanting corporal punishment is a hangover from times past is, frankly, bullshit, whatever psychologists may think. I was at a liberal, progressive school, with no corporal punishment whatsoever, but I spent an awful lot of time wishing I could use my gym shoe on my friends' bottoms, or even be sent to the headmistress's office for six of the best.

I do know where it came from, at least in detail, if not the original urge. I used to read all the old girls' school adventures, and the ones for boys too. In fact, I preferred the boys' ones, because the girls always had it too soft and I wanted to read about whackings and scary masters who carried a cane everywhere they went and used it whenever they pleased. I liked school erotica too, especially if the prefects were allowed to spank, because that is what I wanted to be, head girl in a mixed school where corporal punishment was an everyday occurrence. I even got caught reading one, a really quite smutty one, for which in any proper establishment I'd have been caned in front of the whole school, or at the very least given a bare-bottom over the knee from the headmistress – but no, all I got was an understanding talk and a session with the school therapist.

So that's the way I am, and it remained a fantasy for years, until I found out about the LDS on the net. I already knew that there were such things as adult corporal punishment schools, but they definitely weren't for me. The basic set-up would be some dominant type, or even a pro, who would hire a house miles from anywhere and charge heavy fees for people to come and pretend to be back at school for a week. I couldn't afford it, and because they were so expensive it really was just a handful of old men dressed up as schoolboys. The LDS is different.

Isaac, the guy who set it up, genuinely likes to play at being a schoolboy and isn't out to make a profit, so it's run by the pupils, for the pupils. You can take any role you like, but you do have to accept the rules of play, which are too tough for most people. That means you're subject to discipline from the staff and you can't refuse, unless you have some pressing real-world reason, of course. If you're due a punishment you have to take it, and there's nothing pretend about the punishments.

It has to be like that, for me, because there's no other way of capturing that sense of fear and authority. Once I'm in role, my power is real, and I use it, while there's also the constant fear of ending up on the receiving end. I switch roles, you see, and I do need the occasional spanking or the cane, but only if the circumstances are exactly right. That's why I've taken on the role of a sadistic prefect, so that I can punish as many girls and boys as possible, but with the constant risk of having the tables turned on me. My favourite fantasy is to be overcome by junior girls out after revenge.

There's a system of gangs, you see, and every new pupil joins one, unless they're exceptionally submissive and want to be in trouble from everyone. Most of us are in the gangs, all of which are rivals, and anybody who gets caught on their own by another gang is in real trouble. My gang is Old School, who dress in proper regulation uniform, the way I am now: dark-blue gymslip with the school crest and a chevron if you're a prefect, white blouse, school tie correctly knotted, regulation knickers in white, navy or bottle-green, stockings worn with a suspender belt and plain black shoes with no more than an inch of heel. We use canes, as the correct implement of English corporal punishment.

Then there's New School, who are basically sluts and do things like sucking off the owner of the local Pakistani corner shop to get free chocolate bars. They look more like Richard's fantasy schoolgirl, with skirts so short they're always showing their knickers, blouses half undone and ties loose. The exhibitionists tend to be New School, and there's not much point in spanking them because they love it too much, but if you get caught by them you're likely to end up licking pussy. They spank with their hands and touch you up while they're doing it.

Next is Smart Set, who like to think they're gangsters. They do dress in uniform, sort of, but with blue pencil skirts and tight waistcoats to show off their figures without actually revealing anything. If you get on the wrong side of them you're in deep trouble, because they're into tying up and knife play. They're definitely the cruellest, and they have no sense of fair play, but they do pride themselves on being able to take a lot of CP, so it's fun to break them.

The Heavies really can take it, because to get in you have to be at least five-eight and over twelve stone, and be able to take twelve of the wooden paddle without crying out. Most of them are pretty thick, but they treat everyone else with contempt and like to play cruel games like challenging a girl to arm wrestle, with a paddling for the loser, when she knows she hasn't a chance. I usually avoid the Heavies, because I know that if one of them doesn't want to take her medicine she's likely to dish it out to me instead.

Even worse are Blue Brigade, who're a bunch of fascists with attitude to match. Most of the prefects are either from Old School or Blue Brigade, because we're the only ones who really believe in proper discipline, so they're our particular rivals. They like to use paddles too, but leather ones, and if they get you you're always beaten in public.

Last are the Punks, who're like New School only worse, dirty and slovenly as well as being sluts. They deliberately rip their clothes and some of them don't even bother with knickers or bras. A Punk will usually try to get out of a punishment by offering sex, because they have no self-respect at all, but if you do whack them they always blubber. Getting caught by them is seriously bad news, though, because, while they only use their hands or a shoe at worst, they play dirty – once you've been spanked they might make you lick or kiss their bumholes, or even piss on you.

So that's the set-up, six gangs, each with anything from a couple of girls to ten or twelve, plus a few stragglers and the staff. There are boys too, but most of them cross-dress and the ones who don't have to be stragglers. For staff, at the moment we have a headmaster, a janitor and a cook, so, as you can imagine, they don't have a hope in hell of controlling the pupils. Old School do as we're told, naturally. The rest don't.

Venues are always a problem. When the LDS was first set up, in 1986, it was apparently quite easy to get the use of genuine Victorian schools which had been closed down but hadn't yet been demolished or turned into flats. Nowadays everything seems to get developed double-quick, and it's not so easy. We do have quite a good place in Hackney, which used to be an old theatre or something. There's a single large hall and quite a few small rooms, which are vital if it's going to work properly. An ordinary club with just one huge space is no good at all.

As you can imagine, everybody wants to get their own way, and there's continual plotting and subterfuge between the gangs, and the staff too, who to all intents and purposes are another gang, only we're not allowed to punish them. You see how it works, then, from a D/S perspective? The pure doms are staff, the pure subs are the stragglers, the dominant switches like myself are prefects, and the submissive switches make up the rest. I know some of you may not understand that, and it doesn't really fit in with the conventional view that everybody's either dominant or submissive at heart, but that's bullshit anyway.

The thing I like best is the tension, because you never know what's going to happen on any particular night. We meet in normal life as well, and there are endless intrigues and alliances, while every one of us always has others after her for revenge and still others to take revenge on. You can plan all you like and it can still go wrong, but the most important thing is to make sure your gang is well represented on the night, because, if it isn't, you're in deep trouble.

We have fifteen girls in Old School, which makes us the second biggest gang after New School, but we've never managed to get more than twelve to-

gether on any one night, while last October there were
only three of us. That was a disaster.

In September we'd been the biggest gang there, and
had a really good time of it. We caught some New
School fighting with the Punks and decided to punish
all five of them. With ten of us there was nothing they
could do about it, and we forced them to line up in
the corridor and touch their toes. As the senior
prefect present I decided on the punishment, six of
the best each, so that each of us could give out three
strokes.

We decided the punishment ought to be on the
bare, and my friend Alice had a brilliant idea and
used the safety pins from the Punks' uniforms to pin
up their skirts, all five of them. I then went along the
row and took their knickers down, those who had
any on, so we had five bare-bottomed schoolgirls in
a row, every one touching her toes and looking
seriously worried about what was going to happen to
them.

I made them wait like that for five minutes, and
several people came past, some laughing at them,
some staying to watch the caning. An audience
always brings out the sadist in me, and I made each
girl count her strokes, adding on extra if she moved
or squealed too much, so that one of the Punks had
taken twelve before I was done with her. We finished
off by taking their knickers as trophies and ordering
them to keep their skirts pinned up for the rest of the
evening so that they had to go around with their cane
marks on show.

That left me in the mood for more, but Blue
Brigade were out in force and it's never wise to
provoke the Heavies, so we set about trying to get
one of the Smart Set girls on her own. We almost
succeeded with Leah, the prettiest of them, but she

ran into the kitchen and hid behind the cook, Matt, who's this huge fat guy. He threatened us with a wooden spoon, which hurts as much as the cane, so we had to run for it, but we hadn't given up.

It's always possible to make a deal with the Heavies, so we had Alice go down on Big Eva in return for their help with Matt. He's big and doesn't normally go sub at all, but one of the basic rules of LDS is that if you can't defend yourself you have to take it unless you have a very good reason, and just being dominant is not a good reason. There were seven of them, all big girls, and they managed to get him down. Big Eva sat on his head and the others spread him out, still fighting and swearing revenge, not that you could hear much with her bum in his face, and she must be pushing twenty stone. I could have told him he'd be best off giving in, because they'd only intended to hold him down while we grabbed Leah, but because he wouldn't stop struggling they pulled his legs up, beat him with his own spoon and stuck a sausage up his bum to teach him a lesson.

Meanwhile, we'd got Leah and we decided to make an example of her for running away in the first place. As we were already in the kitchen we had the perfect opportunity, because Matt loves to torture girls and always makes sure he has plenty of nasty stuff around to do it with. As he was currently having his hands tied behind his back with the ripped-up remains of his own T-shirt, he was safely out of the way, so I got the girls to hold Leah down over a table while I searched for what I needed.

It didn't take long, and you should have seen her face when she saw the big piece of root ginger and the bottle of extra hot Jamaican chilli sauce I'd found. She started to struggle again, but that only encouraged the girls and they kept her firmly in place, although I did have to pull her shoes off to stop her getting me with her metal stiletto heels. That didn't stop her kicking and writhing like an eel, which isn't surprising when you consider what she was about to get, but she should have known it would only encourage me.

I pulled her skirt up and took down the fancy French knickers she had on underneath first, to leave her with the shame of being bare for as long as possible, then came around to the front so that she could watch while I carved the ginger root. There was murder in her eyes, and she wouldn't stop swearing and calling for help, so I had Alice give her a panty gag – you know, knickers in the mouth and tied off with a stocking, the way your nurse did you, Richard.

That shut her up, and she could only glare at me as I cut the piece of ginger root into the shape of a small plug, with a round thick end, a narrow waist and a small wider bit as a handle. She knew full well where it was going, and the fear and consternation in her eyes were truly beautiful, especially when I poured some of the chilli sauce on top. Figging, it's called, when you put a piece of ginger root up a girl's bottom before a beating. It's supposed to stop her clenching her cheeks, but it doesn't, not always. It does sting, though, like anything, and so does chilli sauce.

I think Leah must have been done before, because as I went back behind her she was wiggling her bottom in a desperate effort to stop me putting the fig in, but of course she only succeeded in making herself look silly. The others got hold of her legs and pulled her cheeks apart, showing off her bumhole, which was opening and closing because she was so scared. I rubbed a little chilli on her cunt first, then put the fig in, pushing it well up until her bumhole closed on the neck. That's the knack with a fig, you see, to make a tight neck so that it stays in while the girl's caned.

We waited a while for the pain of the ginger root to build up, which was great to watch, because as her bumhole got hotter she started to squirm and kick her feet up and down, until she was going absolutely frantic. I gave her twelve slow ones, each delivered after holding my cane across her cheeks for a while, and twice missing on purpose to make her wince. The last two strokes went across her thighs, which hurts far more than on the bum, and by then her knees had given way, so she was lying limp across the table with her bumhole red and open where she'd squeezed out the ginger root plug. For that I gave her another one across her thighs before we let her go, and she ran for it without even bothering to take her panty gag out or pull up her knickers.

It was late by then, and I knew that if the headmaster found out what we'd done to Leah all ten of us would get the cane, with the whole school assembled to watch us beaten as the finale for the evening. Fortunately, Smart Set aren't sneaks, unlike New School, and we got away with it.

At the next LDS munch we were all talking about what had happened. Leah came and thanked me with a hug and a kiss, telling me I'd taken her as high as she'd ever been, then that I'd better watch it next month. That's how it works, you see, because we'd genuinely scared her, and the pain of being figged and caned was very real – but, as I'm sure at least some of you understand, what seems to be a contradiction is actually the very heart of erotic submission, that you can crave something and hate it at the same time. The knack is to understand your own feelings and accept them.

Whether you can understand or not, I'm sure you can imagine how I felt for the rest of the month. Smart Set were out to get us, and their revenge was sure to be as bad as what we'd done to Leah, if not worse. There was New School and the Punks too, and as the leader of Old School I would be the one they wanted. The last time something similar had happened they'd sent Alice back to us with her hands tied behind her back and her school knickers stuck a little way up her bum so she had a sort of floppy green tail hanging out between her cheeks, but that had been the Punks, who didn't really care who they got as long as they got somebody. Smart Set are more focused.

I was genuinely scared, but that sort of fear is exciting, not at all like when you think there's a risk of something you genuinely don't want, more like the thrill of getting to the top of a curve on a roller-coaster ride. Not that I was going to give in easily, and I spent my time making sure the rest of Old School were coming to the October event so that I'd be safe. As there are only eight girls in Smart Set, including two really wet special girls – that's cross-dressers to you – we might even be able to turn the tables on them. There's nothing funnier than when a girl thinks she's going to get you and ends up getting it herself. They hate it!

Unfortunately it didn't work out that way. There was a cold going around, and I'm still not sure if Leah didn't manage to bribe some of us, but on the evening there were only three of us there, myself, Alice and Miki, who's Japanese – very dominant and pretty tough, but only five foot one, so she's not really a lot of use if things get heavy. Anybody who thinks they can dominate others by pure willpower should try a night at the LDS, believe me.

I knew I was in trouble, with six of Smart Set there, four Punks and seventeen New School. Even if we stuck together we'd had it, and then I found out that Smart Set and the Punks had formed an unholy alliance specifically to deal with me. Blue Brigade would never form an alliance with us, and there were only three Heavies, but I immediately went to see Big Eva anyway, because if the six of us stuck together it would probably be enough.

She agreed, and I went into first lesson feeling relieved, if not exactly safe. In fact, I was so distracted I nearly got called up for the cane by the headmaster for not paying attention, but Alice managed to whisper the answer without being noticed and I got away with it.

The next period was gym, and my heart sank when I saw that I was supposed to be taking it myself, with no staff present at all. We do gym in our school knickers, and a vest if you want, although the sluts from New School and the Punks generally don't bother. That means leaving your implements with your clothes, according to LDS rules, and Old School follow the rules. Smart Set don't.

I found myself faced with all six of Smart Set, in their fancy knickers and silk blouses, every one of them with her knife, as well as the Punks, whose leader, Suzi, was naked but for her school socks and plimsolls, which was somehow even more intimidating than Smart Set. We were still OK, because obviously the knives are only for show and very careful games – or we would have been, had it not been for the deal Suzi and Leah had made with New School.

They came forward, twenty-seven girls to six, and made a very simple demand: that I should be handed over to them without a fight. The others could go free. Naturally no Old School girl would ever accept that, nor any Heavy, and when we told them what they could do with their offer they rushed us. I like to think we put up a good fight, but inevitably we lost, and I ended up with my hands tied behind my back, bent over and attached to the big climbing rope we'd fixed up at the centre of the room.

That position hurts so much. It's all you can do to keep your balance, and of course you're completely vulnerable, while the pain in your arms is usually worse than whatever you get across your bottom. Not this time it wasn't. They took my knickers down and hauled my vest up to leave my breasts hanging out, just to humiliate me even more.

I was beaten like that, first with Suzi's gym shoe, then by Leah with a thick leather strap, 24 strokes each, but that wasn't the worst of it. When they'd finished with me the New School girls took over and frigged me off while they spanked me, in front of everybody else. To be made to come like that may not hurt very much, but it is far more intimate, intrusive really, especially with all the girls looking on and laughing at me because I couldn't help the reactions of my own body.

They'd got Alice and Miki too, although the three Heavies had backed into a corner and were holding their own. Alice was face-down on the floor with girls sitting on her back and legs, her knickers down while they beat her with their gym shoes, and they'd spread Miki out on the mat and stripped her naked with her legs spread while one of Smart Set teased her cunt.

I was let down eventually and, although my bum was covered in bruises, I felt I'd got off quite lightly. After all, I hadn't had anything stuck up me, and they hadn't even done anything disgusting, mainly because most of the Punks had been too wrapped up in trying to get the Heavies down to worry about me.

What I do find, though, is that once I've had something like that done to me I find it very hard to be dominant for the rest of the night. That was just as well, really, because they stripped all three of us and made us go nude for the rest of the evening with our smacked bums on show, just like we'd done to the others. I don't completely agree with you about nudity either, Richard, because once you're in role as a schoolgirl you stay that way for as long as the scene lasts, even if you've been stripped. The only difference is that you feel humiliated. That's the way it works for me, anyway.

I was spanked four more times that evening: once by Big Eva, who felt that what had happened was mainly my fault, once by two Blue Brigade girls who cornered me in the loos, once by Mr Suggs, the janitor – and the dirty old bastard fingered me too – and, to cap it all, by the headmaster, for not being in uniform. The only consolation was that I managed to avoid Matt the cook, because he was too busy trying to get his revenge on the Heavies. By the end I was in sub-space, a sort of natural high you get after being really well dealt with, and so far gone I let Freya from Blue Brigade take me home.

She fucked me with a strap-on, and I freely admit I loved it at the time, but you'd have to be in LDS to really understand the disgrace of giving in to that from a member of another gang, and particularly Blue Brigade. Freya made sure everybody knew as well, by putting it in the circular email sent out before the next munch, so you can imagine how I felt, and how badly I wanted my revenge.

Old School has an honour code, and so I was quits with Leah and the others, but not with Freya and

Blue Brigade. In fact, I wanted revenge on all five other gangs, but I imagined that was too much to hope for because they would always outnumber us so heavily. It was Alice who came up with the idea of bribing the headmaster, Mr Gorleston, which wasn't really Old School style, but was too good to resist.

We have a formula, so that if you want to meet somebody in character other than on an official LDS night you simply text or email in advance setting out the deal. Dave – Mr Gorleston – is very much the old-fashioned headmaster, always in a black suit with a school tie and his Oxford MA gown, which is black with a scarlet silk hood. A suit is a uniform too, in my mind, just as surely any other, and it definitely gives authority. Dave is Dave, just one male friend among many, but Mr Gorleston is a man who can order me to take my knickers down for the cane whenever he sees fit, and I do it.

As you can imagine, it's not easy to bribe some-body like that. The usual currency at LDS is chocolate, that or sex, but it was obviously no good offering him a packet of chocolate buttons to fix the biggest outrage in the school's history. Sex was no use either, because his wife is in New School and, while she's perfectly happy for him to spend his evenings thrashing schoolgirls, they're not swingers, and that works for role play as well as real life.

In the end we had to admit that he was incorrupt-ible, which was when we decided to threaten him instead. The staff know they're at risk, but until then there had always been an unwritten rule that the headmaster was untouchable. I decided to end that, and sent him an email to arrange a meeting, in role of course.

He chose a quiet pub near where he lives, which meant that I had to travel right across London in my uniform. Old School dress properly, so I wasn't indecent, but our style is straight out of the 50s. Even with my coat on I was getting curious looks, but I stuck my nose in the air with true Old School contempt and let them think what they liked.

Mr Gorleston was already there when I arrived, looking frighteningly stern in his suit and gown, and goodness knows what the other people in the pub must have thought when I took my coat off and joined him. Nobody can ever guess my age when I'm in uniform, so it must have looked very peculiar indeed, with a master in earnest conversation with a schoolgirl. Hopefully they thought we were having some kind of highly illicit affair, at least at first.

It wasn't easy to put my proposal to him, not in role. Just to look at him made me feel weak at the knees, but I was determined.

'What is it then, Soames?' he asked, using my play surname, which made me feel even weaker.

'Old School have a proposal to put to you, sir,' I told him, my voice sounding desperately meek in my ears.

His eyebrows lifted at my temerity as he replied. 'Which is?'

This time it took a conscious effort even to speak.

'We want you to punish the entire school, sir, excluding ourselves obviously.'

'Punish the entire school?' he answered, genuinely surprised, I think, before he managed to rally himself. 'That, Soames, is precisely the sort of request likely to lead to me *not* punishing the entire school, excluding yourselves obviously.'

He gave a dry chuckle at his piece of wit. I forced myself to go on.

'I don't think so, sir, because, if you don't, we're going to deal with you.'

His expression changed instantly, first to astonishment and then to outrage. I went on quickly, stumbling over my words as I outlined what we had decided.

'It's very simple, sir. You announce a punishment for the whole school excluding Old School girls. It will be at the beginning of first class, and if you start the lesson without making the announcement we will mob you and give you six with your own cane over the block. We want the punishment given a special way, too. You and Cook and Mr Suggs are to line the girls up around the room, then sit down on three chairs. Mr Suggs is to pin their skirts up to the backs of their blouses and take their knickers down, while Cook and yourself are to spank them one by one. When each girl has been spanked she is to be sent to stand against the wall with her hands on her head and her bottom showing until the end of the lesson.'

He had got over his initial shock while I was speaking, and sat back with a twinkle of amusement in his eye. There was nothing he liked better than to spank girls in school uniform, and my threat was the perfect excuse to do it to maybe as many as thirty. When the alternative was a public caning, I was sure he would make the sensible choice. His voice was level as he replied. 'So you think the entire school deserve to be spanked, except Old School?' he asked. 'Why?'

'Slovenliness?' I suggested. 'None of them dresses properly.'

'That is true,' he admitted. 'Yes, maybe the matter of improper dress has gone far enough, and were I to award a spanking to all those not in correct uniform it would effectively exclude Old School without raising the finger of suspicion in your direction.'

'Good idea, sir,' I said, smiling happily as the tension began to drain from my body. I had done it.

'On the other hand,' he went on, 'I can't possibly allow myself to be dictated to by a pupil.'

'I'm not trying to dictate to you, sir,' I said quickly, 'only suggesting that the rules on uniform should be properly enforced.'

'You are questioning my decision then?' he asked, raising one eyebrow.

I felt myself start to go cold. I recognised the formula, a verbal trap he frequently used when he wanted to punish a girl: forcing her to choose between two options, both of which were insolent, and insolence meant punishment. We were in a pub, though, not a busy one admittedly, but our table was on a raised part of the floor and two bar staff and about half a dozen customers had a clear view of us. He couldn't possibly spank me, not then and there. I relaxed a little and tried to wriggle out of the trap.

'I wouldn't dream of questioning your decision, sir. I think it's a very good decision.'

'So you are trying to dictate to me?'

'No, sir, just . . .'

'I think you are, Soames.'

'No, sir.'

'No? So let me get this straight. Do you think the school dress regulations are too lax?'

'Yes, sir.'

'And whose responsibility is it to see that dress regulations are maintained?'

'Yours, sir,' I answered, hanging my head.

'So you are questioning my decision? Think carefully before you answer, Soames. To deny it would be lying, wouldn't it?'

'Yes, sir.'

'So which would you rather be punished for, Soames, lying or questioning my decision?'

I made a face, then decided to be cheeky and hope he'd forget the incident before the November party.

'Neither, sir,' I said.

'Insolence as well?' he answered. 'Well then, young lady, as it seems you are determined to get yourself punished, I think you'd better come across my knee.'

'What, here? You can't!'

I was so taken aback I'd broken role, but that didn't really matter. A spanked schoolgirl is a spanked schoolgirl, and that was what the other people in the pub were going to see if he had the guts to go through with it. I wanted it, badly, but I was terrified as well, my tummy fluttering and my face on fire at the thought of being punished in public. Finally he answered me.

'Oh, can't I? We shall see about that, young lady. Over my knee.'

Even as he spoke he reached out to take me by the collar, and the shock as I realised he was really going to do it was something close to orgasm. It was awful, so thrilling and yet so shameful that I felt sick to my stomach as I was hauled into place across his knee with my bottom sticking out towards the entire pub. I was babbling out words, but I don't suppose they made any sense, and they ended in one huge choking sob as my school skirt was lifted and my big bottle-green knickers put on show.

And he took them down. He took my knickers down in a pub, where all those people could see – not just my bare bottom, but my cunt lips too, because I've admired my rear view in the mirror often enough to know how much I show. He spanked me like that, not hard, not for long, but he didn't need to. I was a bare-bottom schoolgirl taking a spanking in public, something I'd fantasised about so, so many times.

Now it was happening, and, if it was role play, then the customers didn't know that. For all they knew I was a pupil of his, or even his daughter, and as those ten or twelve firm smacks landed across my bare cheeks I was close to orgasm from the sheer overwhelming head trip of what I was getting.

He was so cool about it too, timing it to perfection. A dozen or so smacks, then he'd covered my bottom, pulled me to my feet, drained what was left of his drink and left, towing me behind him. The bar staff and customers hadn't even had a chance to react, it was so sudden, and they were all staring like so many goldfish as we left, his parting remark floating behind us.

'I'm sorry you had to witness that, but she is badly in need of discipline.'

I tell you, if he'd decided to have me in the street, then and there, I'd have given in, wife or no wife. Fortunately he was in control of the situation and quickly bundled me into a cab. As we drove off I saw one of the barmen come out of the pub, but we were gone, and that was when the reaction hit me. I was shaking uncontrollably and couldn't stop myself. My head was spinning, and every sensation seemed to be magnified a thousand times: the feel of my knickers around the top of my thighs, because I hadn't had a chance to pull them up; my bare warm bottom on the cool leather of the seat; the stiffness of my nipples within the fabric of my bra. I had to come.

'I'm sorry. I can't help it,' I told him, and I spread my legs to show off my lowered school knickers and my bare cunt.

His response was an indulgent little smile and to put his arm around my shoulders. The cabbie couldn't see, or if he could he preferred to enjoy the show rather than object, and I was too far gone to care anyway. Mr Gorleston was holding me as I rubbed my cunt in the back of a London taxi. I was a spanked schoolgirl, masturbating because I'd been spanked in public and I couldn't push away the sexual feelings brought on by my exposure and shame and the pain of the slaps.

I thought of how the barmen and customers must have seen me, a schoolgirl in her old-fashioned uniform, all very demure and innocent, then upended across her headmaster's lap, her school skirt lifted, her big green knickers pulled down and her bare bottom spanked. Those last three words were running through my head again and again as I went through my orgasm, and I don't care what people say or what they think of me, because to be able to achieve that level of ecstasy is worth anything the world can throw at me.

He was so good about it too, holding me tightly around my shoulders as I came but never once trying to interfere with me, although I wouldn't have stopped him. He cuddled me afterwards too, letting me cry my emotions out on his shoulder, which was another wonderful experience, although goodness knows what the driver thought was going on.

After what had happened between Dave and me he could hardly turn down my request, and we would have mobbed him too. So at the November party every single girl except Old School got spanked, on a sort of production line, which they found hideously humiliating and we thought was hilarious. And that's that, for the time being.

Eight

'You're a dark horse, I must say!' I told her. 'I knew you were open-minded, but I never suspected you were into anything like that.'

'It sounds fun to me,' Violet put in. 'How about having a policewoman called one night?'

'We could,' Cathy agreed.

'A nurse would be better,' Kitten said. 'Catch me a pretty girl from one of the other gangs and I'll give her an enema.'

'You're a pervert, Kitten!' Vanity said with a laugh.

'You're all perverts, the whole lot of you,' John put in. 'Not that I mind, but you really are.'

'It's the only way to be,' Kitten insisted. 'So much more fun than boring vanilla, but you lot are so tame! Even you, Vanity. I'll tell you how to get off on being in uniform.'

'And what have you done that's worse than me?' Violet demanded.

'Or me?' Angelique added.

'Plenty,' Kitten replied.

'She does like to give other girls enemas,' Cathy pointed out. 'That's pretty heavy. You were going to tell us how you got your revenge on Vanity?'

'So I was,' Kitten answered as Vanity went pink. 'Thanks for reminding me.'

* * *

If you really like kinky, there no better fetish than being a nurse. It's a licence to do the most perverted things you can imagine, as Sub-Lieutenant Vanity Belle knows only too well. Let's go back to that night, shall we?

I'd heard all about her, how she liked to swank around in her navy uniforms but was a little pussy-licking subbie at heart, and I wanted my share. I thought I was going to get it too, because what she didn't tell you was that we were drinking together in Whispers for more than three hours. I've never come across such a flirty little slut in my life, wiggling her bottom in her white navy ducks when she went up to the bar and looking at me with those big soppy eyes while I talked to her.

She was obviously up for it, and she had me well horny, and drunk too, so by the time I got her back to my flat I reckoned she'd be ripe for an enema and a bit of nursey play before bed. I've had girls like her before, and men, who like their botties smacked but think watersports is too dirty for them, at least until they got a hose up their bums or my pee trickling down their tits. When they find out how nice it feels they soon change their minds, but sometimes you need to be firm with them at first.

That's what I was going to do with our Vanity, and I wasn't surprised when she said she was going to put up a fight, but I thought she just needed to get over herself – you know, feel she'd been forced into it so that she didn't feel bad about getting off on something so dirty. I really thought she'd only put up a token fight, and I never realised the vicious little bitch meant it until she had me on the floor. You all know what happened then, the dirty bitch made me tongue her bumhole.

Not that I care, but if she wanted me to lick her bottom she only had to ask. Why not? There's nothing nicer, just as long as I get the same favour in return, because if there's one thing I can't stand it's people who expect stuff from you but won't put out the same. Not that our Vanity's like that, is she? No, she's not.

She's a little slut, that's what she is, and I knew I only had to take her down to have her doing exactly what I wanted. I'd soon got her sussed too, with her thing about ranks and authority, but a sub-lieutenant's not all that senior. Three stripes and a pair of red shoulder tabs on my matron's uniform and she melted like the little doe-eyed dolly bird she is. I caught her at home, on a Sunday afternoon, gave her a bottle of wine to drink and told her she was due for medical inspection.

There was no fight this time. You should have seen the little poppet, holding up her white uniform skirt to show me her bum, and when I yelled at her to hold her cheeks apart she did it at the double, holding them open to show off her little brown arsehole to the world. Yes, Vanity, in your fancy peaked cap and pretty white uniform jacket, as smart as paint from the waist up, only skirt up and knickers down behind, showing off that same little bumhole you'd made me lick.

I marched her into the bathroom, still holding herself like that, which was just plain comic, and made her stand by the loo while I got her ready. You should have seen her face as she watched. Even as I put my rubber gloves on she looked terrified, and when I opened the pot of lube and stuck my finger in she started to bite her lip and her eyes were like saucers. She kept her cheeks apart, though, and only whimpered a little as I lubed up her bumhole and pushed two gloved fingers well up inside her.

It's always best to lube a girl up before you set up the equipment, because that way she gets a couple of minutes to think about her greasy bumhole and what's going up it while she watches nursey at work. That's how our Vanity was, watching in serious concern while I filled a two-litre enema bag and hung it from the shower rail. Of course, the innocent little poppet had never had an enema in her life, so she was even more scared than she would have been otherwise.

I attached the hose to the bag and put the nozzle on the other end right in front of her face, so she could see what was going up her bum and how the water flowed when I tested the tap. You should have seen the panic in her eyes, but she's an obedient little slut and held her pose, only flinching a little when I touched the nozzle to her bumhole. I'd got down close, because I love to see the way a bumhole spreads and tightens as it's penetrated, and of course our Vanity's a virgin in both bum and cunt, so she's extra tight.

The nozzle went in easily enough, even the wide bit that holds it in place up the bum, and I couldn't resist fucking her with it a few times before I turned the tap on. It's just gravity flow, so it took a moment before she felt the pressure inside her, and then she began to make little shuffling noises, then gasps and this lovely whimpering noise before she started to speak.

'That's enough, Kitten ... I mean Nurse. I'm not sure I can hold any more. Please, Nurse? That's enough. That's really enough. Oh my God, I feel like I'm going to burst. I am. Come on, Nurse, please? I'm going to do it. I am ... It's going to come out, Nurse, all over the floor. Stop, please!'

And all the while she's making these little treading motions with her feet and wiggling her bum, just so cute, far too cute for me to let her off. She likes her military thing, though, because for all her begging and squirming she stayed just as she was, with her hands still holding her bum cheeks apart so I could see the nozzle up her hole and the way her ring had started to push out from the pressure in her rectum. She was trying to hold it tight, and I love to watch a girl's ring squeeze when she thinks she's going to do it all over the floor.

I was nice, though, because she's such a girlie. I turned the tap off as soon as she started to leak and told her to sit down on the loo the moment I took the nozzle out. She obeyed and got down just in time to let it all out into the bowl, and, although she was blushing like a page boy, she couldn't hide the relief on her face, or the pleasure. One of her legs had started to shake and she couldn't control it, always a good sign, and I knew she was mine.

There was no complaint and no resistance as I slipped a hand down between her thighs, and as I cuddled her to me her face went straight to my chest. I opened the front of my uniform a little to let her get to my titties, and do you know what the little slut did? She pulled one out and started to suckle on me while I frigged her off, and this with her bumhole still wide open and her enema dribbling out. What a slut!

Yes, you can very well go pink, Vanity Belle, but you told them how you spanked me and how I licked your arse, didn't you? No complaints when you get a dose of your own medicine, then. Oh, yes, you can bet I made her return the favour too, still seated on the loo in her pretty uniform, with her head up the back of my skirt from behind and her tongue doing the business on my pussy and between my cheeks. She's a good little bum licker, our Vanity, and she really knows how to make a girl come.

That's Vanity Belle dealt with, and don't take any notice of her protests, because if she didn't like it we wouldn't have been lovers for six months, would we? Seriously, though, she's a sweetie and I wouldn't have her any other way than dirty and a switch, because I do like a good thrashing, and to see her in her white navy uniform makes me want to melt. Do you know she beat me over a cannon once? It was in Cornwall, where the old forts that used to guard the harbour at Falmouth have cannon in place as if they were still in use.

You can imagine what that did for Vanity's naval fetish, so we came up early one morning, me naked under my coat, and she made me strip and straddle one of the cannon and then beat me with a cat-o'nine-tails. She took pictures too, the little pervert, and when I'm not around she likes to bring them up on her monitor and rub her little cunt over them. You do, don't you, Vanity? There's no point in denying it. Kissing the gunner's daughter, she called it, but I made her pay. I had her do drill in her full dress uniform, only with a handful of ice cubes down her knickers. That made her jump to it, I can tell you.

So I suppose you little perverts want to know what I've been up to? OK, I'll tell you, but I warn you I don't hold back, so if you can't handle it you'd better leave now, especially you boys. No? Right.

You saw my act, and you know I like to play at being a nurse, but I kept that tame because Richard didn't want to risk a visit from the boys in blue, Angelique's bare bum notwithstanding. Normally I play hard, and I agree with Violet that the more real the play, the better. Like Violet, I used to be for real, and like Violet I soon found out that real uniforms and kinky sex don't mix.

I was brought up a good Catholic girl, under a name I haven't used in years and would prefer to forget. Schooling never really took with me, and, while I get the idea of Cathy's fancy role play, I could never ever get off on pretending to be a schoolgirl again. I got out as quickly as I could, and because I needed to support myself right away I got a series of crappy jobs I won't bore you with before winding up as assistant deputy charlady's dogsbody at a convalescent home on the outskirts of Dublin.

It wasn't the most amazing of places, but after my school it seemed like paradise. What it wasn't was well paid, but there was at least a small clothing allowance and I had to wear a starched pinafore coat with a broad belt, just like the nurses' uniforms only all white instead of pale blue, with a white belt, or all blue for sister. I liked that uniform, because for the first time in my life it made me feel as if I mattered.

I quite liked the job too, because both the other staff and the patients were generally nice to me and I don't get icked out by stuff. I don't mind sex either, because at my school it was considered unmentionable, so I didn't even get the usual guilt trip. I wasn't naïve, though, because I knew what boys had that girls didn't, and I also knew what boys like girls to do, dirty little bastards that they are.

So, when the first guy at the home tried to get me to toss him off when I gave him his bed bath, I did it, and I charged him a fiver. It got me off, actually, because I like handling cock, and I especially like handling cock when I'm in control. When a bloke's got one leg in plaster he can plead and bully and offer to pay me all he likes, but the final choice is down to me, and I loved the sense of power that gave me right from the start.

Word soon got around among the patients that I was good for a toss and a grope of my bum, or even a blow-job if they were really lucky. That I hadn't done before, and the first time was weird. I think I'd been tossing off Mr Somner and old Mr Ferguson for a couple of weeks before Mr Morris asked if I'd do him. There was no danger of getting caught, and he was half stiff already just from having me sponge him down, so I took him in hand and soon had him wanked up and hard.

He was bigger than the other two, and very pale, with a thick foreskin, so I could make the head pop in and out while I wanked him, which was fun. I was sitting on the bed while I did it, and he'd started to grope my bum through my uniform, so I told him I'd let him put his hand up my coat for an extra fiver.

'How much to take me in your mouth then?' he asked.

I was a bit shocked. This may seem stupid, but I thought the fantasies I had about allowing a man to put his penis in my mouth were just a product of my filthy mind. Surely nobody really did that stuff? I kept my cool, though.

'Ten,' I said, 'or fifteen if you want to feel my bum while I do it.'

'Up your coat?' he asked.

'That's twenty.'

'Done.'

So I sucked him off, and, if having a man in your hand gives you power over him, then it's ten times more with your mouth around his cock. I love it too, the taste, the feel, everything, but that day I was thinking how the nuns would react to seeing me, just the way they thought was right for me, at the bottom of the ladder doing my shitty job in my little white uniform, only with a big fat cock in my mouth while I got my bum groped under my clothes, and loving every second of it.

That was Mr Morris. Counting him I was servicing three men, two in my hand and one in my mouth, but they talked to each other, and before long I was sucking them all off and had offers for more. I had to work out a price list, because they used to get pissed off with me if I charged differently for the same thing, but I always tried to be fair. They used to start to get stiff when I washed around their cocks anyway, so I kept it at a fiver for a hand job, as a sort of basic service, which I must have done every day, four or five times, for over a year. I still love it when they start to groan and maybe say dirty things to me, and then the little white fountain of spunk comes out. They're just so helpless.

I made it twenty for a blow-job, which may sound greedy, but, believe me, if you have to suck three men in a row it really makes your jaw ache. They could touch my bum through my coat anyway, but it was an extra fiver if they wanted to go under my clothes. Some just liked to squeeze my bum, or pat my cheeks, but most of them liked to get dirty and tickle my hole or put a finger in me. The only thing I wouldn't let them do was my cunt, because I still believed my virginity was precious, although fuck knows why. What does it matter if somebody's been there before? Men!

All of that was pretty safe, because there were no carpets on the floors in the corridors and I could hear anyone approaching. Men used to get hard when we gave them bed baths anyway, so, if anybody did come in, an erect cock was no big deal, just as long as I wasn't sucking on it and the guy's hand wasn't up my coat. I had to mop up quick when they spunked, but even that wasn't too big a problem. Nurses have to be practical, and men get hard and men spunk up. That's just the way it is.

What was risky was showing my tits, and as I've got big ones a lot of the men wanted to see them and have a grope. That was OK through my coat, but if they wanted to get me bare I had to undo at least three buttons, which were great big white things, and not easy to do up quickly. That's why I charged an extra tenner for a quick feel or a suck of my nipples, and thirty to do it tits-out or give them a titty fuck.

Mr Sugden was the great one for titty fucks. He used to make me sit astride him with my coat pulled up and my top three buttons undone so I could pop my tits out of my bra and rub them in his face, before going down lower and squeezing them around his cock to make a slide so he could fuck in my cleavage. That was really risky, because it meant my back was to the door and I had to concentrate on keeping my titties around his cock properly, and making sure I didn't get any spunk on my uniform. He was worth it, though, and one of the few who'd leave me wanting to go and rub my cunt in the staff loo when I was done with him.

Pretty soon I was making four or five times my proper wages every week. It was a private home, so most of the men who went there were pretty well off, but they had nothing to spend their money on except me. I learnt an awful lot about men there, too, mainly that, however rich or powerful or successful they are, underneath they're all dirty little boys. Men like routine too, although each of them has his own peculiarities. Old Mr Ferguson used to like a hand job three times a week and a suck on Sunday morning before they wheeled him down to chapel, and he'd always come with the top joint of his little finger up my bumhole, never any other way. I cried my heart out when he finally died.

Then there was Mr Barker, who used to make me take my knickers off under my coat and tidy up his room like that, not that he could see anything much, other than the backs of my legs, but he just liked to know I was bare. Some men prefer legs anyway. Mr Adams used to make me roll my coat up so it was like a miniskirt, with the full length of my legs showing, and he'd have me sit on the bed like that, with my legs crossed so he could look at them while I tossed him off.

They came and went, of course, although we did have a few resident patients who only went in a wooden box, like poor old Mr Ferguson. Most would stay about two weeks, but they soon got to know that little Kitten who mopped the floors would toss them off for a fiver. It was Mr Ferguson who gave me my nickname, by the way, and I've kept it ever since.

I suppose I was bound to come unstuck in the end, but if it hadn't been for that bastard Eadie I might still be scrubbing floors and tossing off my patients today . . . well, no, I'd probably be sister by now, but I'd still be tossing off my patients. Eadie was one of those stupid, greedy bastards who can't leave well alone. Everyone knew my price list, and that it was fixed unless I did it for free, but that wasn't enough for him, even though he was quite rich. He tried to blackmail me, demanding that I do what he wanted or he would tell Sister. I wouldn't have gone with that anyway, because I'm stubborn and if you push me I'll only push back, but he wanted to fuck me, and he knew I was a virgin because a lot of them got off on that. That was the deal, my virginity for his silence, so I told him to fuck off, thinking he'd back down because if he got me sacked he'd get nothing. He was a vindictive bastard, though, and told Sister, but on the quiet, so that she crept up and caught me giving Mr Sugden his weekly titty fuck. We'd just finished, so there I was with my little white uniform open and spunk all over my tits. I got the sack.

Fortunately I had upwards of twenty grand in my account by then, and nobody knew about it, so I buggered off to England double-quick. There was a weird time after that, because I didn't really know what to do with myself, but what I did discover was that a year and a bit of tossing off dirty old men in my nurse's uniform had left me completely fixated. To me, that was sex, pure and simple, and as I lay in my bedsit with one hand down my knickers my thoughts would always go to something I'd done, the dirtier the better, like having my bumhole fingered while I sucked on Mr Morris's fat white cock.

I wanted more, and more of the same, but it wasn't so easy. I could hardly ask for references, after all, but I did at least have some experience and finally managed to get myself signed up as a trainee. Now that was weird. I was living in a huge nurses' home attached to St Barnabas in Cardiff, with great long corridors and lines of doors all the same. It was hard work and quite strict, with endless rules and regulations, all in the name of health and safety.

It was completely different from Dublin. All the men were in wards, most of them were too ill to want what I could offer, and there were no opportunities anyway, but what I did discover was the joys of lesbian sex. I wasn't completely innocent, but I'd never gone further than a kiss and a feel of each other's tits, so Leila came as a bit of a surprise, a nice surprise.

She's five years older than me, and I suppose she must have picked me out as a slut, either that or as too lonely and naïve to put up any resistance. Not that she had much trouble. I was fascinated by her jet-black skin and the way she smelt, but most of all by her natural authority. She was a fully qualified nurse, which meant a blue uniform with a white belt, almost exactly like the ones in Dublin, so I suppose it's no surprise that I felt she should be giving me orders, but she seemed to have the same effect on everybody else too.

I was in white again, which had the effect of keeping me more or less permanently horny – not really what you want when you're trying to learn a trade. Leila used to come in and sit on my bed while we talked, and I used to itch to touch her, if only for a cuddle, so there was no resistance at all when one night she slid her hand under the sheets and began to massage my shoulders. It felt nice, a bit confusing too, maybe, because I wasn't sure what she was doing and it was making me feel desperately horny, but when her fingers moved to my breasts I just gave in.

She took me, pure and simple, stroking my breasts through my nightie until my nipples were hard, then pulling it up and kissing them until I was moaning and arching my back for more. My legs had come apart even before her hand went down between my thighs, but I told her to be careful of my virginity. She said she would, but that seemed to make her more eager, just like the men. She spent a long time manipulating me though my knickers and kissing and licking at my breasts and my mouth too, before she peeled the bedclothes down and climbed on top of me.

She stripped me, pulling my nightie and knickers off to leave me stark naked, but she was still in her full uniform and didn't seem to be in any hurry to take it off. I'd have let her do anything, but what she wanted was to enjoy my body and she spent ages teasing and caressing me before going down between my legs. I'd only ever come under my own fingers before, and it was amazing what she could do with her tongue, and how long she was prepared to take over getting me off.

Men are always greedy. Even the ones who like to lick pussy want their cocks attended to pretty much right away, and some women can be just as bad. Not Leila. She spent ages down there, licking and kissing and stroking me with her fingers, until I felt as if I was going to explode. When I did come it was glorious, and she held onto me for ever so long afterwards, before finally demanding her own turn.

I could hardly refuse, and I was willing enough, but I'd never licked pussy before. She gave me a lesson, her knickers and tights pushed down and her uniform rucked up while she sat on my bed with me kneeling at her feet and following instructions. It took me ages to get her there, but she was really patient with me, and quite obviously getting a major kick out of teaching a junior.

That was the start of my first real relationship, and, if tossing off the men in Dublin had got me fixed on being a nurse, then it was Leila who got me fixed on other people being in uniform too. Not that she was particularly into her own nurse's outfit, but she liked to be the one in charge, and that meant keeping her uniform on while I was stripped down. I didn't mind that at all, and she was a good teacher.

I remember the first time she spanked me, and my first ever spanking, erotic spanking anyway. She was ever so gentle, persuading me that it needed to be done and that I would feel better for it, then taking me carefully across her lap and stroking my hair for a bit before she turned up my uniform skirt. I was a bit nervous, because I didn't really understand how punishment could be a part of sex, and I think with anybody else I'd have freaked out. Not Leila.

She took hold of the waistband of my knickers and held them like that while she explained why they had to come down, then peeled them off my bum to get me bare. I could feel myself trembling, and was genuinely scared of the pain, but it wasn't like that at all. She started to stroke me, very gently caressing my bottom for ages before the caresses turned to pats and then smacks. I was soon warm, and I could feel the heat of my bum and the sense of lying across her lap going to my pussy, until I started to moan and push my bottom up for more.

I got told off for that, but only playfully, and she began to spank harder, building up gradually with my excitement until I was getting a proper hard spanking, by which time I was so turned on I was wriggling against her leg and begging her to bring me off. She did it with one hand between my legs, continuing to smack my bottom until I came.

Just as she'd explained, I felt good afterwards, not just because I'd come but something else too, a sense of release. She explained that that was a normal reaction to punishment but that it would be better if she were to take me in hand and give me discipline when she felt I needed it. I agreed, and after that she used to spank me often, hard and without any preparation other than the classic ritual of being put across her knee and having my bottom exposed.

I soon came to crave it, and I still do, especially from a nurse, but any woman in authority is good. It didn't take me long to learn to dish it out either, once I got a little more confidence, and Leila and I used to take turns. It was always me first, and once I was warm and horny I'd return the favour, taking her across my knee to have her pretty blue uniform lifted and her knickers taken down for spanking. She had a wonderful bottom, full and meaty, with smooth dark skin that made a lovely contrast with the big white knickers she liked to wear.

By the time I finished my training I hadn't had any sexual contact with a man in ages. I'd seen them naked, obviously, and given bed baths and stuff, but it wasn't at all like Dublin. At first I was so wrapped up in Leila that I didn't care, but the memories of how it felt to take a cock in my hand or my mouth gradually began to come back, until I was even thinking of it while I was head to tail with my girlfriend.

We never did split up as such, but she stayed on at the hospital and I took a job as private nurse to Sir Conrad Addingham, who has to be about the biggest bastard of all time. I mean, I already knew what men are like, and that if they're friendly it's because they want your knickers down, but he was just plain evil.

I couldn't believe my luck, at first, because the pay was well over the odds and it also looked as if I'd be travelling all over the place. I wasn't naïve about it, because I knew full well he'd chosen me mainly for my looks, not because I was an exceptional nurse. Maybe he had me sussed out from the start, because, to me, being expected to toss him off or suck him or whatever was all part of the job, while most of the girls I'd been at college with would have run screaming at the first suggestion of anything dodgy.

When I turned up at his huge house in the Chiltern Hills I wasn't that surprised to be given a uniform that ended halfway up my thighs, and be told that I was only supposed to wear my bra and knickers underneath. That was a rule, not an option, and, yeah, it should have made me suspicious. There were a lot of other rules too, mainly about how I had to attend to him twenty-four-seven. I wasn't even allowed to speak to other men, outside his staff.

It took me a couple of days to realise what an utter pig he was. He was still in his sixties, and not even all that ill, but I've never met such a hypochondriac. He behaved like a spoilt brat in a grown man's body, constantly grumbling at everybody and threatening us with the sack for the most trivial things. I told myself I'd stick it for a few months and then find an excuse to leave so I could get a decent reference, but things didn't work out that way.

I tried, I really did. I did as I was told and made a little sex doll of myself, bending at the waist to show my legs and being sugary sweet all the time, but that wasn't enough for him. He wanted me frightened of him, and kept barking at me and deliberately putting me into situations in which I would inevitably get something wrong one way or another. At first I thought he was out to set up a situation that would give him an excuse to spank me, and then perhaps make me suck him off afterwards. Even that I wouldn't have minded too much, but it didn't happen. He just seemed to want to put me down, especially in front of other people. I think the idea was to break my spirit, so that when the crunch came I'd do as I was told without making a fuss.

When the gardener, Lee, started coming on to me I took it at face value. He was a big guy, very dark and hairy, and it had been an awfully long time since I'd had any cock. I knew it was a sacking offence, but I needed it too badly, and gave in ... no, I didn't give in, exactly, but the moment he showed interest I had him just as surely as he had me. He wanted to fuck me, but I soon got control and took him in my mouth instead, which was nice, I admit that.

What wasn't nice was discovering that it was all a set-up. I was called up to Sir Conrad's room and found Lee already there, trying not to grin. I was told we'd been seen, and after a bit of bollocks I was given

201

a straight choice: perform for Sir Conrad or get the sack. He thought he had me, and he was already squeezing his cock under the covers and probably thinking about watching me lose my virginity, which Lee had told him about. I called him a blackmailing old bastard, but he wasn't having it, and told Lee to do me anyway.

I really thought I was going to be raped, but fortunately Lee wasn't prepared to go that far and refused to do anything unless I was willing. Not that it would have bothered him to fuck me if I'd been too much of a mouse to refuse the blackmail, but still. Anyway, the old bastard really lost his temper, ranting and raving at us, telling us we had better do as we were told or we'd be sacked.

We were, too, or at least I was. Lee went crawling back to him the next day promising to put his word against mine if I brought an action, and I was out on my ear. And that's the sort of man who runs the country! Women ought to be in charge, we really should, because men are just crap. Look at the mess they've made of the world.

The more I've learnt, the more I realise that's true. Women should lead and men should follow, and be punished regularly to keep them in their place. In fact it ought to be available on the NHS, just to keep the little brats in order. You'd have to report to your local hospital, once a week, where matron would spank you, hard, maybe after an enema. It's what they need, deep down, because men get off on punishment like nothing else. Believe me, I know.

Men need to be humiliated. It does them good, and the more humiliated they are, the better I feel. Spanking's good, because it makes them feel like the dirty little boys they all are, and that includes the three of you, Richard especially. It should always be done bare, with their cock and balls dangling down so everyone can see how excited they get.

What's even better is to fuck them up the arse, or do anything with their arses for that matter, because it feels good and they get horny, and if they're not cool about it they start thinking that it means they're gay, which is just so funny. You seem to think Olivia was cruel, Richard, but I'd have been far worse. For a start I'd have given you an enema before buggering you, and I'd have made you do all sorts of dirty things first, before I even let you come. You'd have done it too, because I'd have had you so high you couldn't resist.

I'm not as bad as her, though, because I wouldn't have left you tied up, and I'd have made you come at the end instead of halfway through. That was cruel. There's nothing I like better than torturing men, except possibly torturing other women, but you have to let them get their rocks off, it's only fair. Besides, make a man come and he's easy to handle.

There are limits, though, and Sir Conrad Addingham was way beyond them. He was a vindictive bastard, too, because he did everything he could to make sure I couldn't get another job, including having me accused of theft. I knew his staff would back him up, so I fled, losing myself in London, where I met Gavin, another prime bastard, who tried to put me on the game.

He didn't succeed, but he did make me realise how I could earn a living, offering sexual therapy as a nurse, which I've been doing ever since, along with a little striptease and burlesque when I feel like it. It's good too, because they absolutely worship me. You talk about army uniforms and authority, but a nurse has far more authority than any army officer. Think about it, how many people have had to take orders from an officer? Not many. Violet's police outfit is better, but it's traditionally a male role.

It's amazing what men will do for me when I'm in my uniform, especially my dark-blue matron's outfit – things they'd never dream of otherwise. It means they can let go, you see, and give in to the things they really want, because they can pretend they're only doing it to please me. I don't let them make the choices. My deal is for them to give themselves over to me completely, which is how it should be.

I advertise myself as a genuine nurse, too, because it's true. I'm qualified, after all. It's just that most nurses don't offer the sort of services I do. They should, though, because if men were punished and wanked off on a regular basis the world would be a much happier place. I get my kicks from it, even if it's just a spanking and a toss, which is my minimum, because I don't let them call the shots any more. It's a good feeling, when you tell them you'll toss their cocks but only after they've been spanked, especially the macho ones, and just about all of them get over their pride soon enough.

That's just the basic, though. I do all sorts of medical play: bed baths, injections, internals and, best of all, enemas. I love giving men enemas, just to see the expressions on their faces as the tube goes up, and then when the water starts to flow and they feel the pressure inside. It brings out the worst in me, I tell you, although what's nearly as good is getting them to do things to each other, especially cock sucking. I tell you, there is nothing, but nothing, so good as to see the look on a straight guy's face when he's got another man's cock in his mouth.

They love it too, so long as they're under my orders and can salvage some pride, but when it comes down to it I reckon most men would like to suck cock if they could get away with it. That's why I offer it as a therapy, you see, because it gives them an excuse to do what they really want. I'll give you a couple of examples.

One guy, let's call him Andy, first came to me in a complete mess with his sexuality. He'd been married five years to a woman who needed his support in everything, but he had started to feel the need to be submissive towards women and with her this was out of the question. For the first couple of sessions I simply talked to him, explaining how our society distorts and prevents the expression of sexuality, and that his urges were perfectly natural.

On the third session I took him across my knee, gave him a vigorous spanking and tossed him off while he lay in place, which had him so grateful he was in tears. That was what he really needed, to be taken in hand by a firm woman, especially a nurse, put in his true place and kept there. I used to spank him twice a month after that, and by doing so satisfied something he would otherwise have been unable to express, which in turn enabled him to keep his marriage going, although obviously she doesn't know about it.

He was easy, strictly spanks and wanks, which is enough for most men, and, while I won't pretend I don't get off on it, I do try not to be too cruel if the poor little babies can't handle it. Another client of mine, let's call him Bob, was very different. He'd been paying for domination for years and only came to me because I was new and young and he thought he could manipulate me.

That's a problem for a lot of men. They recognise their need for submission, but they expect a woman who will do as they want. If they're really going to discover themselves they need to learn to do as *she* wants, and put their own needs aside. That was Bob all through. He sent me a long email in advance, telling me in exact detail how I should dress and how I should behave, which included wearing a full-body leather cat-suit, by the way, and smoking an expensive cigar while he worshipped my bare feet.

Naturally I wasn't having any of that nonsense, especially when a decent cat-suit costs over a grand, and I don't smoke, but I did buy the cigar. When he turned up I was in my dark-blue matron's uniform, which is always the best for unruly little boys. Before he could protest I'd taken him by the ear and dragged him into my consulting room, where I spanked him and lectured him on attempting to manipulate women.

He protested at first, but shut up once I'd forced my knickers into his mouth, and I continued to spank him until he gave in and his cock was hard. By then he'd realised he was getting what he really needed, but that didn't mean the punishment was over, only that I could take my time over it. I let him up and made him strip, as the one thing we saw eye to eye on is that men should be naked in a woman's presence.

Once he was nude I strapped him in place over my whipping stool and gave him a little test to see if he was telling the truth about being sorry for what he'd tried to do. I let him kiss my shoes, then took the cigar out. Sure enough, he began to try to give me instructions again, about how I should sit while I smoked it, although to be fair he did want to call me Matron rather than Mistress.

I wasn't putting up with that, so I lit the cigar, lubed up his bottom hole and inserted it – the right way round of course: I'm not that cruel. You should have seen him squirm when he realised what I was going to do, and the look of humiliation on his face when I took a couple of pictures of him with the cigar sticking out between his red cheeks and his cock half-erect too. That was on his own camera, which he'd brought along hoping to get some pictures of my feet, by the way.

I tossed him off like that, after creaming his cock and balls, with gloves on, of course, which always adds to their humiliation. The cigar burnt slowly down all the while until he'd spunked. Inevitably he was impressed and wanted more, but the battle wasn't quite won. Before his next appointment an email arrived asking if I could be in a rubber uniform. Maybe he was just angling for a better punishment, because I'd made it very clear that I was a qualified nurse and not just a puppet for his fetishes, so I decided to test his limits.

When he arrived he received the standard treatment, being dragged into my consulting room by one ear, spanked with his trousers down and made to strip naked. I then took him into the medical room and hog-tied him on the floor of the shower, face-down with his arse in the air. He was thoroughly enjoying himself so far, and watched with pleasure as I put my gloves on. I took a big scoop of cream and smeared it all over his cock and balls and between his cheeks, rubbing it in and fingering him until he was rock-hard.

I then stopped, leaving him shaking with need and begging to be brought off, but all he got was a lecture on not trying to manipulate me, while I prepared my enema equipment. He knew exactly what I was doing but he didn't dare protest, and of course he knew full well he'd enjoy it in the end. I had to use my widest nozzle, because he was so slippery, but I soon had the water running.

He thought I'd toss him off like that, with the water going in, which men love, but that wasn't what I had in mind. I'd only given the tap a half turn, to keep the rate of flow low, but by the time I'd cleaned up and made myself a cup of tea he was getting in a fine state, wriggling around and begging me to take pity on him. I didn't even bother to watch, but sipped tea in my living room. The noises he was making grew more and more distressed, until finally he gave in.

I then told him the knot on his wrists was a bow and that with a bit of effort he'd be able to pull it open. When I came back in half an hour I expected to find my shower spotless and him kneeling on the floor with his ankles still tied. He made it too, but I beat him anyway, forty strokes of the paddle, then put a new pair of gloves on and made him come the same way Olivia did Richard, by pressing on the back of his prostate gland while I was wanking him.

Nine

I felt my cheeks tighten involuntarily at the thought. It was all too easy to imagine her doing it, but while she was undoubtedly attractive she was also slightly frightening. John didn't seem concerned, his tone dismissive as he spoke.

'Don't any of you get off on normal stuff?'

All six of the girls turned to look at him.

'What?' I asked. 'Are you telling me you don't think they look nice in their uniforms?'

'No, I don't mean that,' he said hastily, 'but they look nice anyway. But why not a cocktail dress, or jeans and a T-shirt? Why does it have to be kinky?'

'Why be boring?' Angelique retorted. 'Uniforms are fun. They take you out of yourself.'

'What's wrong with being yourself?' John asked.

'Maybe some of us don't fit into society as easily as you do?' Violet put in, to immediate agreement from the other girls.

'I like being kinky,' Kitten added, 'and can you honestly say you've never been turned on by what a woman is wearing, or how she presents herself?'

'It's the woman inside that appeals to me,' John insisted.

'Which is why you've been staring at the girls all evening?' I asked.

'I'm only human,' he responded, 'and, OK, you do look sexy.'

'I'm glad you think so,' Violet said archly. 'And how about playing with us? Wouldn't you like Kitten and me to spank you?'

She clicked her tongue on the word 'spank' and kept her eyes firmly on John, who had gone crimson.

'I'm not into all that,' he mumbled.

'Maybe whoever spanked you was no good at it?' Angelique suggested.

'I've never been spanked!' John retorted.

'Never been spanked!?' Violet responded in mock horror. 'How do you know you don't like it then? Just think, two girls on you at once, or three, or four, or six even. What do you say, girls?'

'I say we spank him,' Kitten said, 'and I bet he gets hard.'

She had stood up, and so had Violet. John glanced from one to the other, looking embarrassed and rather unsure of himself. Cathy also stood up, then Angelique, and a touch of panic began to show in his expression, which grew abruptly stronger as both Kiara and Vanity joined the others.

'Come on, girls, this is going beyond a joke,' he blustered. 'Richard, tell them . . .'

'You really should try the experience,' I suggested, amused and a little envious. 'Don't let me stop you, girls.'

'We won't,' Violet assured me.

She darted forwards even as she spoke, making a grab for John's arm. He tried to fend her off, only to have both Kitten and Cathy move in from the other side. I could see he didn't really want to fight back, for all his struggling, and in no time at all he'd been pushed down onto the seat and sat on. Kitten was on his shoulders with his arms in the small of his back, helped by Cathy, while Violet clicked her handcuffs into place on his wrists. His lower body was off the edge of the seat, his buttocks already positioned for spanking, but he hadn't given in.

'OK, OK, I'm sorry,' he tried. 'I apologise, all right? There's nothing wrong with getting off on being in uniform, it's just that . . .'

'Shut him up, somebody,' Violet said casually.

'Sure,' Cathy answered, and reached up under her school skirt.

John twisted his head around and watched in puzzlement as she levered off her knickers from beneath her school skirt. He only realised her intention when she began to roll them into a tight ball.

'No, girls –' he began, only to be cut off as Cathy pressed the wad of cotton against his mouth.

'Pinch his nose,' Violet suggested as John began to struggle once more.

'I know,' Cathy answered. 'I have done this before, you know. Could I have a stocking?'

'Have one of mine,' Angelique offered, watching as Cathy forced her knickers into John's mouth with an evidently practised hand.

'Got him,' she announced. 'Stocking, please, Angelique.'

Angelique had raised an elegant leg and was resting her foot on a chair close to John's head as she peeled down one stocking from beneath her pale-blue uniform skirt. Cathy took it and made short work of tying it off, leaving John silent but for muffled grunts, although his eyes were wide with rising panic.

'Trousers down,' Kitten said cheerfully, adjusting her seat on his back, only for Kiara to interrupt.

'Uh, uh, that's my job, for all the times he's been short-tempered with me.'

'Fair enough,' Kitten agreed, 'and you can have first go at his bum too.'

Kiara ducked down behind John, and I'd never seen so much cruelty in her face as she unfastened his trousers – or pleasure. He began to struggle again as his trousers were pulled down, and he turned his eyes to me, pleading silently. I shrugged.

'You'll enjoy it,' I assured him.'

'Yeah, take it like a man,' Paul said with a chuckle.

John returned an angry glare, which turned to consternation as Kiara tugged his boxer shorts down, leaving him naked behind, with one testicle squeezed out from between tightly clamped thighs. The girls moved in, Angelique and Violet pulling his thighs apart to get a better view of his cock and balls, the others peering close and laughing at the display he was making of himself. Only Vanity held back, hovering at the edge of the group but obviously enjoying the show.

Kiara hesitated for a moment and then began to spank, slapping her hand across his buttocks as a delighted grin spread across her face. I sat back to watch, enjoying the view of a maid spanking a cook, an outrage fully reflected in John's face. There was also a touch of relief, because Kiara wasn't spanking particularly hard and he had clearly realised that, for all the humiliation, he could cope with the pain. Cathy had realised too, and was less than impressed.

'Put some effort into it, Kiara,' she said. 'He needs to be taught respect and then perhaps he'll learn to be less of a git to us. I'm getting a spoon for my turn.'

John gave a somewhat louder grunt as Kiara's smacks grew harder, but otherwise failed to react, presumably unaware of how much a kitchen spoon across the buttocks can hurt. Not that he stayed that way for long, for Kiara stopped and stood aside the moment Cathy came back.

'My turn,' Cathy said happily, and smacked the spoon down across John's bottom.

He jerked so hard he almost unseated Kitten, and Violet had to press down on his shoulders to keep him in place before Cathy could continue. John was wide-eyed with consternation and shock, but I was trying not to laugh as I spoke up.

'Don't be too hard on him, girls. He's not used to rough treatment.'

'He's got to learn his place,' Kitten answered.

'And he deserves it,' Cathy added, but she had begun to spank less hard, instead peppering John's buttocks with rapid gentle taps.

He continued to struggle a bit, and to kick his legs as the spoon smacked down, but it was plain what effect the punishment was having on him: his cock was swelling and growing longer. Angelique and Kiara were standing directly behind him and laughed to see his growing erection.

'You were right, Kitten!' Kiara said. 'He's getting hard.'

'They generally do,' Kitten said casually.

'My turn,' Violet urged.

Cathy applied a last few hard slaps to John's buttocks and passed the spoon to Violet. She was laughing as she began to smack his now reddened cheeks, and after a moment she reached out to take hold of his cock, tugging on it as she beat him. John gave an angry grunt through Cathy's knickers at this new breach of his dignity, but the tip of his cock had begun to poke out of his foreskin and there was no doubting his growing excitement.

'He likes it!' Angelique said with a giggle, and reached out to tickle the sac of John's balls with one painted nail.

213

'Sit on him, Kiara,' Kitten instructed. 'I want to see.'

As the two girls swapped places John made no effort to get up, and a shiver passed through his body as Kitten reached out to squeeze his balls. Violet moved a little to the side, allowing Cathy to squat down and once more begin to spank, so that John now had one girl on his back and four attending to his buttocks and genitals, with Vanity still watching in mingled amusement and disgust.

Kitten took over from Violet on John's cock, tugging it, slapping it and tugging again. He was fully erect, prodding out towards the bench, and his struggles had subsided. Instead he had begun to push down as Kitten masturbated him, only to stop as all six girls began to giggle.

'Who likes his bottie spanked?' Kitten teased. 'And I bet he's thinking about how he's being wanked off by a nurse.'

John gave an angry shake of his head, but Kitten only tugged harder, now pulling on his cock as if she was milking him. Violet and Cathy continued to spank, a buttock each, to a firm even rhythm, while Angelique tickled his balls with her nails.

'Oh, yes, you are,' Kitten went on. 'You're thinking of how you're being masturbated by Nursey while a policewoman and a schoolgirl spank your naughty bottom, aren't you? Don't deny it, John, because I know, and isn't it nice? Isn't it nice to have Nursey wank your dirty little cock while you're spanked? Yes, John, you're loving it, aren't you, and you're going to come over me, aren't you? You're going to come over your nurse, or over Cathy in her school uniform, or over Kiara in her cute little maid's outfit, or Angelique as an air hostess, or maybe Violet, or Vanity. What's it to be,

214

John, a nurse, a policewoman, a sweet little school-girl . . ?'

John gave a violent jerk and came, all over the floor beneath him. Kitten laughed and began to tug on his cock as fast as she could, milking out jet after jet of spunk and Violet and Cathy redoubled the force of the spanking. Powerful shudders were passing through John's body, and when they finally stopped he gave what might have been a despairing groan.

'Schoolgirls,' Kitten said. 'He's into schoolgirls. You're a dirty pig, John.'

Kiara stood up, Violet retrieved her handcuffs and John got unsteadily to his feet, unable to look the girls in the eye as they stood back. He seemed thoroughly ashamed of himself but he made no protest, simply moving off towards the male toilet with his trousers and boxer shorts clutched in his hand. Only when he reached the door did he remove the stocking and Cathy's knickers from his mouth.

'There's one who'll be coming back for more,' Violet said confidently.

'You're not wrong,' Angelique agreed.

'Whose turn next?' Kitten demanded.

She looked at Paul, who merely shrugged his massive shoulders and smiled, then at me. I felt my stomach tighten, but they weren't going to need to spank me to get me hard. I already was, but that was unlikely to make any difference.

Violet had her handcuffs dangling from one finger as she stepped towards me.

'Put your wrists out,' she ordered.

'Make me,' I told her.

'Tough one, huh?' she answered. 'OK, let's get him, girls.'

All six of them came forwards, grabbing my arms and legs to pull me up from my seat and into the middle of the floor. I fought back, just hard enough to make sure they did a thorough job with me, and before they could get a proper hold on my arms I reached up under Angelique's uniform skirt to pull her knickers down.

'You'll suffer for that!' she promised, and then my arms were dragged back and the cold metal of Violet's handcuffs clipped into place across my wrists.

I was eased down to the floor, still struggling even as Cathy straddled my body. She twitched up her school skirt, showing her bare bottom, which she lowered towards my face.

'I seemed to remember he likes this,' she said, giggling, and her warm fleshy cheeks settled onto my head, spreading to leave my nose up her bottom and my mouth pressed to her pussy.

As I began to lick, my legs were being held out and my trousers unfastened. I couldn't see who was doing what, but they made short work of it, stripping me naked from the waist down.

'Who's a bad boy then?' Kitten said, as my erect cock was taken in hand. 'Already hard, I see?'

Cathy had begun to wriggle her bottom in my face as my legs were hauled up and open, exposing me completely. Kitten continued to tug on my cock with the same clinical efficiency she had used on John, while another girl began to spank me with the spoon. It stung, leaving me writhing and all six of them laughing, until the warmth began to grow.

I could do nothing, utterly helpless as they amused themselves with me, my tongue well in up Cathy's cunt, my cock hard in Kitten's hand, the spoon smacking down on my buttocks. One of them began to tickle my balls, probably Angelique, and I gave in completely to the pleasure, thinking of the six of them; a naval officer watching me punished, my own maid holding my legs up while a policewoman spanked me, a pretty schoolgirl sitting on my face, and a nurse and an air hostess masturbating me. It was too much to resist and my cock jerked in Kitten's hand as I came beneath a pile of girls in uniform.

nexus

The leading publisher of fetish and adult fiction

TELL US WHAT YOU THINK!

Readers' ideas and opinions matter to us so please take a few minutes to fill in the questionnaire below.

1. Sex: Are you male ☐   female ☐   a couple ☐?

2. Age: Under 21 ☐   21–30 ☐   31–40 ☐   41–50 ☐   51–60 ☐   over 60 ☐

3. Where do you buy your Nexus books from?
☐ A chain book shop. If so, which one(s)?

_____

☐ An independent book shop. If so, which one(s)?

_____

☐ A used book shop/charity shop
☐ Online book store. If so, which one(s)?

_____

4. How did you find out about Nexus books?
☐ Browsing in a book shop
☐ A review in a magazine
☐ Online
☐ Recommendation
☐ Other _____

5. In terms of settings, which do you prefer? (Tick as many as you like.)
☐ Down to earth and as realistic as possible
☐ Historical settings. If so, which period do you prefer?

_____

☐ Fantasy settings – barbarian worlds
☐ Completely escapist/surreal fantasy

- ☐ Institutional or secret academy
- ☐ Futuristic/sci fi
- ☐ Escapist but still believable
- ☐ Any settings you dislike?

_____

- ☐ Where would you like to see an adult novel set?

_____

6. In terms of storylines, would you prefer:

- ☐ Simple stories that concentrate on adult interests?
- ☐ More plot and character-driven stories with less explicit adult activity?
- ☐ We value your ideas, so give us your opinion of this book:

_____

_____

_____

7. In terms of your adult interests, what do you like to read about? (Tick as many as you like.)

- ☐ Traditional corporal punishment (CP)
- ☐ Modern corporal punishment
- ☐ Spanking
- ☐ Restraint/bondage
- ☐ Rope bondage
- ☐ Latex/rubber
- ☐ Leather
- ☐ Female domination and male submission
- ☐ Female domination and female submission
- ☐ Male domination and female submission
- ☐ Willing captivity
- ☐ Uniforms
- ☐ Lingerie/underwear/hosiery/footwear (boots and high heels)
- ☐ Sex rituals
- ☐ Vanilla sex
- ☐ Swinging
- ☐ Cross-dressing/TV

☐ Enforced feminisation
☐ Others – tell us what you don't see enough of in adult fiction:

_____

_____

_____

8. Would you prefer books with a more specialised approach to your interests, i.e. a novel specifically about uniforms? If so, which subject(s) would you like to read a Nexus novel about?

_____

_____

_____

9. Would you like to read true stories in Nexus books? For instance, the true story of a submissive woman, or a male slave? Tell us which true revelations you would most like to read about:

_____

_____

_____

10. What do you like best about Nexus books?

_____

_____

11. What do you like least about Nexus books?

_____

_____

12. Which are your favourite titles?

_____

_____

13. Who are your favourite authors?

_____

_____

14. **Which covers do you prefer? Those featuring:**
    (Tick as many as you like.)

☐ Fetish outfits
☐ More nudity
☐ Two models
☐ Unusual models or settings
☐ Classic erotic photography
☐ More contemporary images and poses
☐ A blank/non-erotic cover
☐ What would your ideal cover look like?

_____

15. **Describe your ideal Nexus novel in the space provided:**

_____

_____

_____

_____

16. **Which celebrity would feature in one of your Nexus-style fantasies?**
    We'll post the best suggestions on our website – anonymously!

_____

THANKS FOR YOUR TIME

Now simply write the title of this book in the space below and cut out the
questionnaire pages. Post to: Nexus, Marketing Dept., Thames Wharf Studios,
Rainville Rd, London W6 9HA

Book title: _____

NEXUS NEW BOOKS

To be published in January 2008

BLUSHING AT BOTH ENDS
Philip Kemp

Funny, full of surprises and always arousing, this is a brilliant collection of stories about innocent young women drawn into scenarios that result in the sensual pleasures of spanking. It features girls who feel compelled to manipulate and engineer situations in which older authority figures punish them, over their laps, desks or chairs.

£6.99   ISBN 978 0 352 34107 5

NEXUS CONFESSIONS: VOLUME 2
Various

Swinging, dogging, group sex, cross-dressing, spanking, female domination, corporal punishment, and extreme fetishes . . . Nexus Confessions explores the length and breadth of erotic obsession, real experience and sexual fantasy. This is an encyclopaedic collection of the bizarre, the extreme and the utterly inappropriate – the daring and shocking experiences of ordinary men and women driven by their extraordinary desires. Collected by the world's leading publisher of fetish fiction, this is the second in a series of six volumes of true stories and shameful confessions, never before told or published.

£6.99   ISBN 978 0 352 34103 7

If you would like more information about Nexus titles, please visit our website at www.nexus-books.com, or send a large stamped addressed envelope to:
  Nexus, Thames Wharf Studios,
  Rainville Road, London W6 9HA

NEXUS BOOKLIST

Information is correct at time of printing. To avoid disappointment, check availability before ordering. Go to www.nexus-books.com.

All books are priced at £6.99 unless another price is given.

NEXUS

☐ ABANDONED ALICE	Adriana Arden	ISBN 978 0 352 33969 0
☐ ALICE IN CHAINS	Adriana Arden	ISBN 978 0 352 33908 9
☐ AQUA DOMINATION	William Doughty	ISBN 978 0 352 34020 7
☐ THE ART OF CORRECTION	Tara Black	ISBN 978 0 352 33895 2
☐ THE ART OF SURRENDER	Madeline Bastinado	ISBN 978 0 352 34013 9
☐ BEASTLY BEHAVIOUR	Aishling Morgan	ISBN 978 0 352 34095 5
☐ BEHIND THE CURTAIN	Primula Bond	ISBN 978 0 352 34111 2
☐ BEING A GIRL	Chloë Thurlow	ISBN 978 0 352 34139 6
☐ BELINDA BARES UP	Yolanda Celbridge	ISBN 978 0 352 33926 3
☐ BIDDING TO SIN	Rosita Varón	ISBN 978 0 352 34063 4
☐ THE BOOK OF PUNISHMENT	Cat Scarlett	ISBN 978 0 352 33975 1
☐ BRUSH STROKES	Penny Birch	ISBN 978 0 352 34072 6
☐ BUTTER WOULDN'T MELT	Penny Birch	ISBN 978 0 352 34120 4
☐ CALLED TO THE WILD	Angel Blake	ISBN 978 0 352 34067 2
☐ CAPTIVES OF CHEYNER CLOSE	Adriana Arden	ISBN 978 0 352 34028 3
☐ CARNAL POSSESSION	Yvonne Strickland	ISBN 978 0 352 34062 7
☐ CITY MAID	Amelia Evangeline	ISBN 978 0 352 34096 2
☐ COLLEGE GIRLS	Cat Scarlett	ISBN 978 0 352 33942 3
☐ CONCEIT AND CONSEQUENCE	Aishling Morgan	ISBN 978 0 352 33965 2
☐ CORRECTIVE THERAPY	Jacqueline Masterson	ISBN 978 0 352 33917 1

NEXUS CONFESSIONS

NEXUS ENTHUSIAST

- - - - - - ✂ -

Please send me the books I have ticked above.

Name   ....

Address   ....

....

....

.... Post code ....

Send to: **Virgin Books Cash Sales, Thames Wharf Studios, Rainville Road, London W6 9HA**

US customers: for prices and details of how to order books for delivery by mail, call 888-330-8477.

Please enclose a cheque or postal order, made payable to **Nexus Books Ltd**, to the value of the books you have ordered plus postage and packing costs as follows:

UK and BFPO – £1.00 for the first book, 50p for each subsequent book.

Overseas (including Republic of Ireland) – £2.00 for the first book, £1.00 for each subsequent book.

If you would prefer to pay by VISA, ACCESS/MASTERCARD, AMEX, DINERS CLUB or SWITCH, please write your card number and expiry date here:

....

Please allow up to 28 days for delivery.

Signature ....

Our privacy policy

We will not disclose information you supply us to any other parties. We will not disclose any information which identifies you personally to any person without your express consent.

From time to time we may send out information about Nexus books and special offers. Please tick here if you do *not* wish to receive Nexus information. ☐

- - - - - - ✂ -